GREETIN

My name is Ap
Planet Reginta.
I would like to thank my esteem   e,
collaborator, and friend, J. Jack Bergeron, for
helping me write this book.

Appleton

Website: j-jack-bergeron.com

Other books by J. Jack Bergeron:
50,000 A.D. The Awakening

PLEASE BEGIN READING HERE

You are one brave person for purchasing this book.

You might have heard rumors of certain dangers in the reading of it, but I want to dispel this immediately. The nanobots that are stored in this book are in no way harmful. As you open the pages, they instantly begin to penetrate your fingers. After you finish reading, they quickly leave your body once you remove your fingers from the designated pages containing the story of this book.

My name is unpronounceable in your audible language, so I have assigned the easy to pronounce name of Appleton for your edification. Believe it or not, our species communicates with each another using parts of the electromagnetic spectrum typically in the infrared and radio wave region. Our physical bodies actually produce these waves, and this has come about by a crazy evolutionary system that happened in two stages. You will learn more about that as you read this book.

I know you'd like to begin reading, so let me give you a few instructions before you proceed.

1. Owning this book allows you the privilege of traveling to our home planet Reginta by using nanobots residing in the pages throughout it. Do not oppose these nanobots; allow them access to your body.

2. Once the nanobots are flowing, they will connect your mind with an avatar located on Reginta. When this happens, please relax, as this will allow you effective control over it.

3. Even though Reginta is about 16,000 light years away, this operation will be done in real time, so do not feel worried you might be out-of-sync with your local situation for long periods of time; you will not. Our technology is so advanced, it allows us to transport your thoughts across vast distances almost instantaneously. You

may remove or put your fingers back onto this book anytime you want, as they will reconnect you with your avatar immediately.

Follow the above instructions diligently, and no harm will come to your body or mind.

We first discovered your planet about 50,000 of your Earth years ago. The diversity of life and the fact there was an intelligent species living there fascinated us. It immediately became a source of study, and we chose to keep a close eye on it to see if its intelligent species would gradually become civilized.

As you can tell, you did become civilized. You are reading this book aren't you?

Sometimes it was frustrating following your development. There were times when we inadvertently exposed ourselves, and you began to worship us. When you got out of that phase, you proceeded into the airship phase, then the flying saucer phase, then the Roswell phase, and then the crop circle phase as well as the UFO abductions phase.

These mysteries have subsisted in human consciousness throughout recent history and are some of the reasons we have decided to reveal ourselves using this book. The alternative would be to enter into your main nation's capitals in huge spaceships causing all kinds of panic and maybe even wars among yourselves. You are a bit unpredictable you know. We are hoping this method will be rational and civil, and prevent paranoia or violence of any kind.

Later, we will formally announce on the television networks encompassing your planet that we are here to meet with you and become your friends. This proclamation should not meet with too much irrationality as we expect this book will have conditioned a large part of the world by then.

Another thing I would like you to be aware of, is that in no way do we intend to exploit the resources of either

4

your planet or solar system. We can get anything we want all over the galaxy and have no need of any material things from your area. For the time being, we invite you into our Earth museum, located on our home planet, using nanobots and an avatar reserved for your use.

Now let's get on with reading this book.

Please either turn the page with your index finger and thumb or drag it with your thumb on the paper stock with your four fingers on the cover. For those of you who have an electronic reading device, a finger swipe on the screen or the button that advances the pages will allow the relevant nanobots to proceed into your body.

Please let your mind relax. The nanobots are now flowing through your fingers and finding their way into your brain. Do not feel anxious or nervous, as this will impede the actions you are about to witness.

I am going to ask you to do something that might sound silly. Pretend your eyes are closed; this will help you daydream this experience. That's better. The nanobots should have reached your brain by now, and the story is about to begin.

As mentioned previously, the correct way of describing what this book does, is that it links you to an avatar. You are still physically on Earth, but we will allow your mind to control the avatar just as if it were your own body. As long as you continue to hold the book or reading device, you will be able to see our planet and particularly this museum.

You are now pretending to open your eyes to observe a landscape on a planet in a star system that is about 16,000 light years from Earth. The landscape is rather hazy and is specifically designed to appear Earth-like as a way to ease your possible apprehension.

A human-like person is approaching you. This is our greeter. He will direct you to our museum where you will meet some important people who have interesting stories to tell you. You will also meet a member of the Reginta Brotherhood, the planet's central authority. This unique group of individuals will inform you of all the visits to your planet we have made, including the ones that people have claimed to be UFO visits from outer space all these years.

Before we continue, I have a few things to discuss. The first thing is human beings' sense of humor. Our species doesn't have any. However, we have learned to understand and appreciate this human peculiarity. When we 'get the joke', there is no emotional response or subconscious desire to laugh. We are incapable of laughing at any rate because of our different physiology and decide the 'funniness of a joke' in an intellectual way and over thousands of years, have learned to 'get' almost any joke in any language from human beings . . . almost.

So if you try to communicate with the greeter, do so in your own style and friendliness, but if he doesn't laugh or smile at your humor, don't be offended.

Here he comes. He will extend his hand in friendship as is the custom on your planet, and when he does, please listen to him. As far as the greeter is concerned, what he is seeing is an avatar of you (with clothes on of course). He will attempt to speak to you in the language of the country you come from. Listen carefully, and I will tell you what to respond.

"Greetings Earthling; welcome to Reginta."

Just relax, and I'll control the nanobots in your body to respond as long as your mind doesn't try to oppose them.

OK, here goes: *Thank you for your welcome; I am so happy to be here.*

See, that wasn't hard. Now please follow him.

"Come with me this way Earthling. By the way what shall I call you?"

Now it's your turn to take control of the nanobots. Tell him your first name, or I mean think it.

OK, go ahead . . . Ah . . . I don't think he heard anything. Try it again; remember to relax and not be too nervous.

. . . Hmmm . . . You don't appear to be doing too well. Never mind, there are people who have already been here and have had the same problem controlling their nanobots. The greeter will understand.

See, he hasn't heard a thing from you but still has a pleasant disposition doesn't he. Just continue to follow him. He is now leading you to the central doorway of our magnificent 'Intelligent Earth Museum'. We began building this about one hundred of your Earth years ago. This place is the focus of our efforts to bond and make friends with you Earthlings.

Since you appear to have trouble speaking, he will point the way to the exhibits. They begin in the corridor to your right. If you notice the greeter, he is indicating a place for you to sit down, so you can watch a visual about us and our relationship with human beings. This will take about 60 of your minutes.

By the way, if you wish to take a break from reading this book to do whatever, now is the time. When you put it down, the nanobots will immediately rush out of your fingers then come back and continue where you left off when you pick the book back up.

This book is divided into four parts that can be read separately.

The 1st part consists of: Who are we? What are we like? and What do we want?

The 2nd part is how we discovered Earth and a brief history of our visits and observations until the end of the nineteenth century.

The 3rd part deals with the 20th century and some unfortunate incidents when humans came into contact with us.

The 4th part deals with our official communication with all your societies including our experiences with both the Democratic and Republican parties in the United States.

I'd like to point something out to you. We will be using a different font for anyone who is communicating with you throughout these pages other than me. This is to make sure that you are not confused when you put the book down, pick it up again later, and then forget who was doing the presenting.

You will be meeting twelve presenters (including me) either live in person, or on a recorded video. Here are their names:

1. Appleton, 2. Tasall, 3. Icecifer, 4. Farlee, 5. Evilochets, 6. Eubas, 7. Tejago, 8. Foduenow, 9. Lovelylosa, 10. Hescute, 11. Erborite, 12. Rukey.

As you can see, it comes out to twelve people. I am only mentioning this because some of you visitors were curious to know if the number twelve is significant in our culture. I can understand that beliefs in Earth based scriptures among religious people can be thought provoking, but please realize that this group of twelve is a complete co-incidence and has nothing to do with the number twelve in historical references like the twelve apostles, twelve tribes of Israel, twelve disciples of Christ, twelve signs of the zodiac, and twelve days of Christmas.

(Some wag here at the office noticed that if these names are arranged in a certain way, they spell out 'THE AFTERLIFE')

One other note: Please realize that this is not a science fiction book or novel. This is real. The planet Reginta is real. I am real. When you have finished reading it, there will be no doubt in your mind whatsoever.

If you found this book distributed in a science fiction area of a bookstore, it is merely because the distribution company has advised us that is the best way to increase sales. We are attempting to list it in all genres possible.

And now, on to Part One.

PART 1: WHO ARE WE? WHAT ARE WE LIKE? WHAT DO WE WANT?

Let me introduce you to Tasall, the tour guide for this part of the museum. Hanging on the wall right before you is a video display that Tasall will use from time to time. Tasall, this is the current human from Earth, so without further ado you may now begin the presentation.

Enjoy!

Hello Earthling, my name is Tasall.

From what I understand, you are having difficulty communicating with us because of uncooperative nanobots. Don't worry, the majority of Earthlings coming here with avatars are not use to it and sometimes can't get into the swing of things. This happens frequently and as long as I know you're comfortable, our session should proceed rather smoothly.

Let's begin with the first point of Part 1:

WHO ARE WE?

We are one of two intelligent beings in this part of the galaxy. We have traveled about half of it cataloging life everywhere and unbelievably, have discovered only one intelligent species other than us. You humans are the other one.

Our ancestry goes back about 1,000,000 years. That is to say, we became intelligent about 1,000,000 of your Earth years ago. Life on our planet of Reginta began about 8 billion years ago, and it took a long time to produce an intelligent species.

From your point of view, this planet is situated in the Omega Centauri Globular cluster and orbits a star somewhere in the middle of it. As to whether we are more intelligent than you are, this debate has been going on for years on our planet. But, we do seem to have a larger memory capacity.

WHAT ARE WE LIKE? - PHYSICALLY AND LIFE STYLE

We average about the same height as humans and have four appendages. The difference is that all four appendages serve the same function. They are interchangeable in their functionality and can be used for either grasping things (like your hands do) or walking (like your legs). We have a total of six eyes, no neck to speak off, and six fingers on each appendage: three of them are thumbs. Our spectral range is superior to yours: all the way from radio waves to ultra-wave.

This is also how we communicate. We converse with one another by emitting photons from three of those eyes. When we are close to one another, the infrared part of the spectrum is used, and when far away, the radio-frequency part. Which we decide to use depends on communication objectives. The RF is utilized when communicating far away or through obstacles, and infrared frequencies when privacy is desired with someone in your vicinity.

SEX

Having only one sex, we do not have sexual partners as you do. When reproducing, we do so collectively and decide as a group how many new life forms to produce. It's a combination of resident demand, clan requirements, population density, and rivalry among planetary systems.

The biological material used in reproduction is placed into follicles on our head with our own hands until one or more of those follicles become pregnant. Those expectant follicles are then removed, placed in incubation chambers, and within a few months, a full sized being is born. There is no childhood as you Earth people call it.

As far as any enjoyment is derived from our biological bodies, yes there is pleasure just like when humans have sex. Under the right stimulus, these follicles receive a type of enjoyment similar to the sexual pleasure you humans have with the opposite sex.

More discussions on this matter will appear throughout this book.

NATIONALITIES AND GOVERNMENT

Like humans, we have different nationalities but in our case, we all speak the same language. There are occasional rivalries among these groups but for the most part, we do get along. Nine official nationalities make up our species, but the Brotherhood have bestowed the right to only one to explore and research planet Earth.

Only one central government composed of representatives from all these nationalities make up our political order. There is no democracy. We never heard of, or even conceived of, this type of government until it emerged from your ancient Greeks and then later in the eighteenth, nineteenth, and twentieth centuries, it began to spread all over your planet. Your experiments with this form of government peaked our curiosity as some of our intellectuals have asserted that it should be examined to see if any of it is applicable to our own cultures.

COMPARING HUMANS AND REGINTIANS

Having a lot of similarities and differences, our intelligence is the one thing we have in common. Since we have better memories, we do very little reading and or studying, and as soon as we acquire even the smallest of facts, we never forget them. For example, studying for an exam to obtain a college degree requires a lot of work for you humans; where with us, when we read things once, that's it; no more study is required.

On the other hand, humans are extremely creative. Just look at the incredible exponential surge in science and technology since your renaissance period especially during the 19th and 20th centuries. Our desire to acquire scientific knowledge was more linear, and it has taken us much longer.

ENTERTAINMENT AND SPORTS

I have already mentioned sex, so let me discuss other things like entertainment and sports. 'Formal' entertainment is something we also have; some of what entertains us is studying you humans and basically studying anything. We do not have sports or 'physical' rivalries in the manner you have. If we do have a sport between individuals and/or groups, it is the accumulation of knowledge.

That doesn't mean that we don't take an interest in your sports. Many of our people living on Earth and the Lunar-Base follow a variety of human sports. The most interesting one for us is anything to do with racing. This is a simple enough concept for us to understand, and we follow all types of racing from the Olympics to wife carrying.

RELIGION

This is an introduction to the differences and similarities between our religions. If you find religion boring you can skip this section, but you might have trouble later on in understanding certain concepts throughout the entire book. Here is a list of what we have in common.

We both worship/pray to the same past and present spirits: Zeus, Jupiter, the Abrahamic God, Hindu gods, Shinto gods, other gods, saints/prophets/angels etc. All spirit worship done by humans and Regintians began the same way; for example:

- 'In the beginning', the spirits brought forth all manner of miracles to entice both humans and Regintians to worship them.

- Miracles are created by placing illusions in the minds of both humans and Regintians.

- The mind is controlled by using multi-dimensional nanobot components that cannot be detected by human technology . . . yet.

- This method can be very effective with small groups of people but when extended to large groups, it becomes unreliable and certain amounts of people remain unaffected.

Regintian technology eventually detected these nanobot apparitions when researching the afterlife: more on that later.

In the past, both humans and Regintians have had the same controversies:
- Rivalry among religions, sometimes war.
- Skeptics not believing in the spirit world.

The following is where we have different experiences with spiritualism and where Regintian religious philosophy is unique.
- There is no more atheism since there is now scientific proof of God's and the spirit world's existence.
- Mortals are not required to worship Spirits. A concession was made to former atheists allowing them into heaven without having to worship any spiritual entity, including God.
- Requirements for entering heaven are itemized in a treaty because previously, religious documents allowed wide interpretation and sometimes cruelty in determining conditions for entry into heaven. Since various events and procedures were always disputed among religions and eras, the treaty finally sorts things out.

- Regintian mortals have the technology to visit heaven but not without permission (the first time they visited there, they sneaked in).

In essence, we both worship the same spirits even if they have different names depending on religion, race, culture, and species (by species I mean you humans and us). There is only one 'set' of spirits existing in the universe, and they are in the line of fire, so to speak (worship that is), constantly receiving prayers from all mortals.

For example, if a human is a Christian one day and converts to the Shinto religion the next day, those two religions will state that they are worshiping different gods and even get into a debate as to whether the 'rival' God/gods are real. The God/spirits in both those religions are in fact the same God/spirits so when you switch religions, you may be told you are worshiping a different god, but those same spirits are still there on the receiving end of your prayers behind the scenes. This is something we were able to determine a long time ago with scientific accuracy.

Incidentally, spirits do not receive a 'type' of energy from prayer; it is ultimately an ego gratification ritual (at least in my opinion).

Let me now discuss our religion specifically.

GOD

The first thing to do is discuss whom this Being is. When comparing our concept of god with the human version, there is a little confusion. Do we have many gods or just one? If you compare our religion directly with Christianity for example, you could say we have one God. If you compare it with the ancient Roman and Greek religions or other existing polytheistic religions in present day Earth, then we have many gods.

I have to admit, this might sound a bit confusing for you. It is probably a result of your rigid stance on what constitutes real and false gods. Most Christian religions, as well as Muslim and Judaic, state there is one God and that is the one they worship.

The ancient roman religion stated there were many gods but only one chief deity named Jupiter (or Zeus for Greeks). The current present day Hindus state almost the same thing except that all of the gods they worship are different manifestations of the same God. You Christians (or some of you Christians -- not all of you) also pray to prophets and saints. When we studied these Christian religions, we couldn't see the difference between praying to a prophet or saint, or to a secondary god in some ancient or current religion. Doesn't praying to a saint or prophet make that person a god? What's the difference between praying to the god of wine for example, or to a saint? Don't they both have the same hierarchy and therefore the same rank within a Christian, ancient or polytheistic religion?

I know this can be confusing, but no matter: we're going to clear this matter up right now. We are going to call these entities -- God, gods, angels, saints, prophets etc. -- The Congregation of Spirits.

Here are some important things to realize:
- We both have the same spirits watching over us.
- There is a central most powerful spirit who is referred to as God (capital 'G' for both of us here).
- Other spirits can be referred to as secondary gods, angels, saints or prophets. It makes little difference what they are called; it's the same hierarchy for all religions.

You humans are still required to worship God, but we are not due to a treaty we signed with Him, which I will explain later.

There are many different religions on Earth and many different gods, and that is the way it use to be on Reginta. The same spirits that we have in our religion are present all over Earth, and we have learned it is extremely difficult to get everyone to worship in the same way when you have such a multitude of languages and cultures having evolved over many tens of thousands of years. Historical and cultural influences are excessively complicated and much too emotional to get everyone worshipping the same way. So Regintian philosophy promotes the idea of letting people worship the way they aspire since they all direct their prayers to the same spirits in the multi-dimensional continuum universe.

I will now discuss why the previous multi-religion state changed on Reginta.

THE HISTORY OF OUR RELIGION

In ancient times, many different cultures and races encompassed our planet of Reginta. The history of our religious beliefs is almost identical to humans. These beliefs began long before we ventured into outer space and went as far back as our own hunter/gatherer epoch. We had many different religions, and they all appeared to be worshiping different spirits.

There were religions that believed only one god existed, some believed in many gods but worshiped only one, and some worshiped all gods. As our knowledge of science and technology advanced, we began to view religion the same way humans currently do now.

Then the big breakthrough occurred: scientific progress sent us to the stars. This led a group of our scientists to devote many years researching the spirit world on a remote planet in a far away system. The spirits were unaware this research was going on. Contrary to conventional thinking, the spirits and/or God don't really have the ability to see everywhere in the universe. That's just a myth believed by humans in the present and Regintians in the past.

Once the breakthrough happened, those scientists suddenly appeared in what humans and Regintians refer to as heaven. How do mortals, created with elements and molecular compounds, have the ability to appear in the spiritual realm?

It is by using what you humans call an avatar. These special bodies have both physical and metaphysical properties. What these scientists discovered was the fact that the spiritual world existed in another series of dimensions, which all the elements in the universe have. The Earthling hypothesis of string theory is at the very beginning of these discoveries. All matter in the universe, including the atoms in your body, exists in many dimensions and once you thoroughly understand it, you can develop methods of traveling into the spiritual world: a power only the spirits have had until this discovery.

I am privileged to be a direct descendant of the expedition leader that first went into the heaven/spiritual universe. His name is Qaddy, and the following are exerts from his very detailed notes on this important breakthrough:

When we arrived in heaven, the Congregation of Spirits were completely shocked. Despite their formidable power, they did not see us coming. However, we were able to avoid conflict on that first day when we both realized this discovery of ours was inevitable. Let's face it, as science and the knowledge of the universe continued to move forward among Regintians, it was likely we would eventually figure out the multi-dimensions of the spirit world.

That, they did see coming, what they didn't envisage was our surprise entrance.

On that particular day, a special five-person avatar shuttle entered heaven for the first time. The first thing we became aware of was our passage in a space that was completely white with no frame of reference for determining whether we had any velocity at all. When we looked outside the shuttle through our viewers, we observed strange objects like the mystical shapes you would expect to find in a spiritual world. A certain fear crept over us as our shuttle continued to wander about this strange universe.

Then suddenly, vibrations shook the shuttle so much, it felt like it was falling apart. Having very little choice, we energized a dangerous shield to surround the shuttle. This was designed to protect the ship against almost any threat, but was a bit destructive if anything approached it. As soon as I turned it on, the vibrations stopped.

When the co-pilot checked the outside of our shuttle, he noticed that a landscape had appeared and looked solid enough to land on. It was obvious these spiritual entities could manipulate matter much better than we could and make any type of solid object suddenly appear no matter how big or small.

During the time these methods were being research by us, some of our scientists thought we would eventually be able to construct things and landscapes in the spirit universe (later on this research would be forbidden in the Treaty of Spiritual Truth). This manipulation of multi-dimensional matter cannot happen in normal 3D space even with all the implied power of the spirit universe.

In the meantime, we received a message from these entities; not through communications equipment, but in our minds. The message was in our language with perfect pronunciation. While we have no recording of it unfortunately, it said something similar to this:

"How did you Regintians enter this space?"

My answer: "We have developed technologically advanced equipment that will now allow us to visit heaven."

There was silence for a moment as the entity pondered what to say.

"Would you mind following us to a place where we can communicate more effectively? It will be safe for you there."

I went along with his request but didn't really have to do anything as the existing landscape we were in *disappeared, and something new appeared. The new landscape conformed to a typical Regintian wilderness countryside. Initially it was devoid of people. Then a person emerges and stands outside our shuttle about ten meters away. My co-pilot and I went out to meet him.*

The first thing I said was, "Are you God?" I could tell from his demeanor and response that he could not read my mind.

His answer was, "That depends." Hmm . . . why was his answer so ambiguous?

"Depends on what?" I said.

"It depends on your disposition towards idealistic concepts."

"What do you mean?"

"If you want to believe I am God, then that is your right to do so, to bring you comfort."

"But I don't care about my comfort, just the truth."

"The truth is whatever conforms to what your beliefs are about life and the tranquility of the universe."

"You can't be God because you sound so confusing, and God is supposed to be perfect and therefore not confusing."

"Maybe a perfect being is also a confusing being."

At the back of my mind, I was wondering if this confusing dialog would continue to be fruitless or was there any grand awareness to be had at the end of it.

"I thought confusing things were imperfect and non-confusing things were more perfect," I said.

"But is a non-confusing thing closer to the truth? I mean non-confusing things might be so complex they could be beyond your comprehension and therefore you wouldn't be able to even consider that you were hearing the truth. Conversely, a confused state would make sure you would likely ask another question which would mean you still had hope of finding the truth rather than giving up in a state of total confusion."

At this point, I gave up so I said, "Are we allowed to explore this area."

He responded, "That depends. . ."

I listened for him to finish the rest of his statement, but all he did was walk away. We decided to follow him. I notified the rest of the shuttle crew to stay put.

Even though I couldn't see anyone at all, I sensed the presence of entities and spirits. I had a feeling their mood wasn't particularly friendly. It felt as if they were displeased about our surreptitious entry into heaven without the effort they had put into getting here.

Suddenly, something weird happened. The sky went black. The God person stared at me with an angry look on his face.

"How dare you."

"What do you mean?" I said.

"How dare you make the sky black like this," he said.

"I didn't do anything," I said with an innocent look on my face.

He pointed to our shuttle, and I instantly knew what he meant. I called the shuttle officer and asked him if he knew what was going on.

"I am sorry Qaddy, I inadvertently had some bad thoughts and the shuttle android read them and mistook them for an order to turn the sky black."

That was an interesting example of how advanced our technology had become since it could read our own minds and turn the sky black in the spirit world without them knowing it would happen.

"Make sure nothing like that ever happens again," I said sternly.

The God person looked at me and said, "I hope this is not an example of things to come. Are you an arrogant Regintian or a peaceful one? We in heaven have to determine what your unexpected appearance might do to our peaceful ways." The sky turned white again. There were obviously many things to discuss.

As I mentioned before, no one up here (up in the usual traditional heaven sense) knew we were coming despite all the incredible power we had attributed to the spirit world since the beginning of our intelligent existence. The more familiar I became with this spiritual existence, the more I found out that they were not as powerful as I thought. The familiarity with their 'habitat' was now in our realm of knowledge: not a very comfortable position for the God person.

The rest of our stay in heaven involved meetings about deciding what to do regarding our newfound knowledge of them. As of our last get together, the God person suggested I go back to my universe and urge our authorities (the Regintian Brotherhood) to have a series of introductory meetings leading to major negotiations later on. Many things needed to be resolved: What were the rules going to be? How does one now get into heaven? How does one go to hell? Will guardian angels continue to have access to all Regintians? There were so many things to discuss and thrash out.

We went back to Reginta, explained everything to the Brotherhood, and returned to heaven with a new delegation. During the course of these discussions, our negotiators had many lengthy confrontations with these spirits. Despite the conventional wisdom that God is supposed to be the most powerful entity in the universe and the most supreme of all the spirits, He still has to seek the opinion of the rest of the Congregation -- if only for political harmony. At the end of these long and time-consuming negotiations, which lasted several months, we eventually produced a treaty.

But it wasn't easy. The first group of negotiators we sent were scientific types who were usually atheistic (or used to be atheist and are now believers) and had their own way of initializing communications with spirits. Here is a typical example of an opening meeting.

A Regintian scientist would begin a negotiation with an opening speech that sounded something like this:

"We are most grateful for this invitation into your realm and look forward to the prosperity that our two peoples will achieve in the future." As you can see, he more or less considered our two groups as being equal in their rights to prosperity, something an advanced mature *race of people like us would have achieved and evolved to a long time ago.*

The spirits on the other hand, would say something similar to this:

"We are delighted that Regintians are about to witness the incredible happiness and enlightenment of achieving a place in heaven, for which you have worked so hard, by worshiping our Lord and doing His will. We have come to the conclusion that despite your mortal predisposition to sin and succumb to temptation, you are willing to cast aside all this enticement and give your whole being and will to the lord God almighty."

After that was said, the 'mortal' scientists sat there quietly, wondering if the 'dispensing' of any rational thinking would actually lead them anywhere.

Well . . . it didn't.

Almost every negotiation began with a long prayer that lasted about an hour and other discussions of any particular detail usually had prayers buried in them. Here's an example.

Mortal: "If and when a mortal -- whether he's previously been an atheist or not -- arrives in heaven, how long will it take to achieve the happiness as stipulated by religious traditions that have existed all these past times."

Spirit: "A mortal entering this hallowed space will have achieved a holiness never felt before in his physical life and will be blessed for all eternity. This eternity will be easily achieved as the former mortal worships and prays to His most Highest Lord and that in itself will bring eternal happiness." A three-minute prayer is said at this point.

Mortal: "Thank you but . . . we wouldn't mind having a bit more detail."

Spirit: "All details, all conclusions, all endings, all accomplishments, will be achieved in heaven as your happiness and praise of the Lord is brought to light and fulfilled."

This first negotiation session lasted about ten days, and in general, the scientists weren't too sure if it had in fact ended. The spirits talked as if it had, but the mortals couldn't note one thing on their list of specific goals they thought should have resulted from all this.

In the end, things were still very polite between the two groups, but the scientists concluded they had gotten nowhere, and left. The spirits told them how happy they were and mentioned to the mortals that all they had to do was pray and everything would be fine in the end. They were quite contented that everything was resolved.

The mortals went back to Reginta and after updating the Brotherhood with all the details, the strategy was changed. The Brotherhood decided to send their most religious thinking people to see if they could do better. They were instructed to play along with the religion-speak (of which they were expert at) but to make sure real official agreements were postulated in writing.

They were gone for one month. When they came back, they had no agreement or treaty but had acquired 192 new prayers and told us we were to teach and dispense them all to Regintians.

"Why did you go along with this?" we asked our confused representatives -- there was no answer.

A more rigid procedure was obviously required for future meetings that took into account all of the spirits' peculiarities. So we arranged a new meeting.

There was another little problem. It had always been a "fact" that the spirit world knew exactly what was going on in the "mortal" world all the time. The reality is this. The amount of knowledge the spirit world has of the mortal world depends on the amount of guardian angels (as opposed to standard angels) that are available for any particular group of people. The vast majority of information about individuals is gathered through these particular 'angels'.

If there are no guardian angels present, then the nanobot option is used. This option is not ideal as nanobot swarms can get lost and fulltime standard angels are required to control them. The nanobots are not an entirely reliable method of gathering information from the mortal world and the chances of obtaining it is vastly reduced. They are strictly a backup option.

For example, if the authorities who organize our meetings are sure the attendees are free of guardian angels, then there's a 90% chance of keeping that meeting secret from the Spirit Congregation. The other 10% of the battle is to keep out the nanobots, which would require building a shield. We were now on the cusp of utilizing a new technology that detected if any individual had a guardian angel and whether nanobots were present.

Once these angels were detected, we diverted the people containing them into a prayer room and after prayers were said, dismissed them. Those people were not told about the real meeting, so no information was fed back to the Spirit Congregation.

This brought up another little discovery. In the past, we always assumed every mortal had a guardian angel; this isn't true. It depends on the supply. Most of the time heaven couldn't meet the demand for these angels. Their basic nature was the reason for this. Essentially, a guardian angel is a being that has passed away in the mortal world and has to stay in purgatory for a while. The so-called suffering the former mortal undergoes is being a guardian angel for a certain period of time. When that stint is over, he is removed from purgatory and is allowed into heaven. If people live longer or forever, then there will be a shortage of guardian angels, and it will be hard for God to keep track of everybody.

So it was a bit of a surprise to discover that only 10% of our invitees to the meeting had guardian angels, not 100% as had been anticipated. Building a shield around the meeting place might have sounded ridiculous many years ago before we 'broke' into heaven. In those days it was felt, 'how could you prevent the spirit world from eavesdropping?' Since we now understand about 'Multidimensional Yieldable Apparitional Space', we can *build shields that prevent spirit observations. The meetings were now spirit-free and could proceed without a feeling of spiritual intimidation.*

The next step was to study the records of that last Congregation negotiation spree with the intent of communicating more effectively with these entities next time.

Some points we emphasized:
- *Do not try to outwit them even if we are tempted to do so.*
- *Do not give up if all you hear is continual praying and Lord praising; just keep pressing rational points.*

When we went back for the third session, we noted an attitude change. They weren't so rigid in their thinking this time. We later found out that their inability to penetrate our shield when eavesdropping on our meetings astonished them so much, it convinced them to view us in a much more serious light.

These negotiations continued for another month until we agreed on what procedures to utilize and set of laws to follow when dealing with any aspect of our relationship.

For example:
- *The spirits did not want any of us to enter into their realm unless it was by their rules.*
- *The mortals longed to end millenniums of misinformation, hypocrisy, cruelty in the name of justice and confusion, about different gods and/or sub-gods/prophets/saints etc.*

That was my ancestor Qaddy, and the agreement he is referring to is call the 'Treaty of Spiritual Truth'.

Here are a few of the major ideas promulgated in the treaty:

Regintians are not required to worship Spirits (including God) anymore. This is a concession to atheists (which comprise about half of Regintian society) since they weren't used to worshiping to begin with.

The idea is this: since these atheists would have a hard time 'getting back into the swing of things' and begin worshiping all over again, the worshiping requirement was dropped. Because of the clear-cut scientific proof of God and spirit's existence, we do not have any more concepts of atheism.

Mortals visiting heaven without permission is not allowed anymore. No more surprise visits like our first one. Requirements for getting into heaven are itemized in the treaty since in the past, religious documents allowed wide interpretation and sometimes brutality in determining these requirements (usually death requirements).

Here is a summary of the most important clauses in the treaty.

TREATY OF SPIRITUAL TRUTH

1. There is no more requirement to worship or pray to anyone in the spirit world including God.

-This clause pertains only to Regintian mortals and does not exempt other intelligent races (if ever discovered) from worshiping spirits.

-We mortals from Reginta will not interfere in the Congregation of Spirits relationship with other intelligent races if and when they are ever discovered.

i.e. obviously this clause was written before we discovered humans.

2. Mortals will be allowed to visit heaven and leave under the following conditions:

- Heaven is located at the center of the Milky Way Galaxy

i.e. called Monderland Galaxy in Regintian

and mortals will have to travel there and back at their own expense.

- The heaven authorities will not be responsible for avatar shortages due to periodic demand.

i.e. Sometimes there will be an excess of avatars, sometimes there will be a shortage.

3. The spirit world will be responsible for issuing only one bible as opposed to a large number under the following conditions:

- The bible will be documented in this treaty.

- What is a sin and what is not will be meticulously spelled out.

4. Hell will be abolished for all Regintians.

- Mortal sinners will simply die and become non-existent.

Regintian science is so advanced, the number of Regintians who die is a very small percentage. As alluded to before, this has created a shortage of souls in purgatory, which means there is far fewer guardian angels than normal.

So it became a reasonable proposition to remove suicide from the mortal sin category, and those who do it will be punished with a one year stint in purgatory and assigned the duties of a guardian angel. This is a major concession to Regintians and a problem solver for the Spirit Congregation. Before this agreement, all people who committed suicide went to hell and were not available for guardian angel duty, now they are.

5. No research or investigations to alter multidimensional matter in the spiritual universe are to be attempted by mortals.

6. Mortals will now be officially kept up to date on the number of sins and their different types in their 'soul spreadsheet' which can be downloaded anytime -- please note that the Spirit Congregation is not responsible for the download time which could be up to thousands of years depending on where you live in the galaxy. To avoid this long period of time, it is suggested that mortals visit heaven to inform themselves directly.

For humans later on, the average 'soul spreadsheet' containing all the sins the average Earthling has had over his lifetime is so big, Microsoft Excel (in the Office app) would not be able to hold all the data. The Windows 8 version might be able to do it, but we didn't have any spy-bots located at Microsoft this time, so we're a little behind in our information.

WHAT IS IT REALLY LIKE IN HEAVEN?

I have traveled to heaven, and I want to give you a very clear-cut view of what it is like, with all its peculiarities. This heaven is the same for all religions whether you're from Earth or Reginta. Since we can now meet with our spirits, we can find out what they do in heaven.

They reside in a storage facility that can house trillions of spirits. How large is this container? This is hard to explain. To be able to determine the size of anything you have to compare it with something: a ruler, yourself, any object you can think of. Since there is no standard physical three-dimensional matter in the spirit world, then there is no standard object to compare to. The spirit world can be the size of the entire universe or the size of a pinprick -- if I can use a standard human viewpoint. What do they do while in there?

Basically nothing: Again, they have eternal happiness and reside in heaven, so why bother doing anything. If they do something they like outside the container, they're happy; if they don't do anything, they're still happy. What are some of the things they could do outside of it?

29

Meet with visitors from the mortal universe. If mortals desire to meet with these spirits, they have to use an avatar. The same type you the reader is now using when viewing Reginta and this museum. If these spirits don't want to meet with you in your avatar for whatever reason, they can stay in their container and since they're in heaven, have the usual eternal happiness.

Heaven is in a specific area of the Milky Way Galaxy, but it is also in a dimensional continuum that has so far only been hypothesized as a theory you Earthlings refer to as string theory. You might get a chance to visit this universe if you read this book carefully, and follow any instructions you happen to come across.

I will turn you over to my colleague Icecifer, who has a simplified explanation of the spiritual existence of the universe. It is extremely interesting, and I highly recommend all visitors pay careful attention.

Hello, my name is Icecifer, and I demand your absolute attention to this matter. I have been told you humans have inferior intelligence, and your attention span is downright delinquent. Depending on your brainpower, I am offering three different explanations.

The first is for those people whose intelligence is below average. The second is for average intelligence, and the third is for above average intelligence. For those who have below average intelligence please read the following very slowly. I am going to deliberately use extremely simple words and mathematically easy equations.

In string theory, Earth scientists have come up with 11 dimensions; we say . . . nice try.

The actual amount is:

11 times the Planck's constant of $6.626068 \times 10{-34}$ m2 kg / s times the speed of light in a vacuum 299,792,458 m·s−1 times the Newtonian gravitational constant of

6.67384(80)×10–11 m3·kg–1·s–2 times the reduced Planck constant of 1.054 571 726(47) × 10–34 J·s.

Once the above factor is calculated, it is divided by 7, then multiplied by 13, then divided by 5125, then added with 666, and then divided again by 444.

This is the complete equation:

$$\frac{\dfrac{\left(\left[\dfrac{11 \times 6.626068 \times 10^{-34}\ m^2\ kg\ /\ 1 \times 299,792,458\ m\cdot s^{-1} \times 6.67384(80) \times 10^{-11}\ m^3 \cdot kg^{-1} \cdot s^{-2} \times 1.054\ 571\ 726(47) \times 10^{-34}}{7}\right]\right) \times 13 + 666}{5125}}{444}$$

When this is done, it should not be repeated verbally.

If it is, it would be in violation of sub clause 5.324 of clause 33 in section 39 of the Treaty of Spiritual Truth.

This is what we consider the basic spiritual constant of the universe commonly referred to as 'Multidimensional Yieldable Apparitional Space', or MYAS for short.

The Second explanation is for humans of average intelligence.

I am assuming you people have a background in gross-dimensional-interspatial-mathematics.

This will actually simplify the explanation.

We begin with the same amount of string theory dimensions, 11, then multiply that by the huberistic-factoral constant (7.777777) then divide it by the saturistic-factoral constant (7.777776) and then demultiply (demultiply means multiplying it in 1/4 of a second) by the hyperdimen-factoral constant (6.777777).

If you have trouble with your demultiplication techniques, then I suggest you practice them before you tackle the above calculations. If you still can't get it done in less than a quarter of a second, then your answer might inadvertently guide you to that other spiritual existence of hell (which still exists for human beings even though Regintians are exempt).

I was going to explain the third way for extremely intelligent humans, but I think I will skip this since this explanation is so complex that the probability of any human, no matter how intelligent, in acquiring the correct answer is approximately one over the Planck's constant to 1.

$$\frac{1}{1.054\ 571\ 726(47)\ \times\ 10^{-34}}$$ to 1 probability of success.

Getting the wrong answer will reserve you a place in hell (again, only if you are human).

Thank you Icecifer.

Getting back to the first simple explanation, this basic equation, along with shall we say -- heavenly technology, allows us to travel all over the galaxy by various means and methods.

The following is a basic table that will give you an idea of the different ways of travelling to heaven (which is located in the center of the Milky Way Galaxy).

Physical methods (other than death)
Methods of travel . . . Time to heaven from Earth
1. standard speed of light . . . 27,000 years
2. hyper-quad-dimensional direct-express . . . 200 years
3. hyper-quad-dimensional com-stream . . . 100 years

Spiritual methods
1. MYAS communication . . . real-time
2. MYAS physical . . . 1 year

<u>VISITING HEAVEN</u>

There are two methods. The first is relatively easy but arduous. A standard inter-galactic cruiser is taken

to the Galactic center where God and the Spirit Congregation have chosen to live. Then one books oneself into a hotel (or with friends if you happen to have them on the local planet) and orders an avatar since they are usually in stock at this location.

Why is it arduous? From Earth it takes approximately 200 years to get there and 200 to get back if you use standard hyper-quad-dimensional direct-express technology -- something we developed a long time ago. We use this same technology when traveling to Earth.

The second way is to stay on your home planet and use an avatar, just as you are doing right now visiting this museum. This might take a while for Regintians since the demand for avatars on Earth is way up, due to the sales of this book you're reading. There are not enough avatars to go around for both Regintians and humans. Humans have the priority since the plan to officially meet them is now in effect.

MORE ON REGINTIAN SUICIDE

I would like to apologize for bringing this gruesome subject up again. Regintians have a completely different outlook about suicide as compared to before the discovery of the spirit universe. Current human thinking about suicide is how we use to feel about it before that momentous event.

Our lives are now quite long since acquiring the biological technology that theoretically allows us to live forever. I mention 'theoretically' because living that long allows us to question whether we actually desire it. After one or two thousand years, a tiny minority of our people want to commit suicide, do their time in purgatory, then proceed to the spiritual universe in the Galactic Center, while others have their minds conditioned to prevent them from doing it. However, most people prefer to live forever.

Incidentally, even though people do commit suicide for the purposes of going to heaven, it is such a small amount that God is actually considering increasing the time in purgatory for these people, so He can meet the demand for guardian angels. The problem with this plan is that it might be a further incentive to not commit suicide, which could result in an even more reduced supply of guardian angels. This has created quite a dilemma no doubt.

Before permanent life appeared on our planet, we normally died of old age or disease or were killed to enter heaven, just as you humans presently do. When one dies, the spirits controlling the so-called afterlife evaluate your soul, which exists in a different dimensional continuum in your body. Those spirits decide whether you qualify to enter heaven or hell (before it was removed for Regintians). If your soul spreadsheet has too many bad entries, into hell you go. If it has above the maximum to enter hell but below the minimum to enter heaven, purgatory is your only option. Otherwise, zero entries allows you direct access to heaven.

Please be aware that all of these procedures happened long before the discovery of Earth. Until we discovered Earth, even the Spirit Congregation didn't know it existed. When it was discovered, and later when Earthlings became religiously aware, the spirits reinstituted suicide as a mortal sin on Earth and committing it condemned them to hell, or so most of your religions state.

This would reinvigorate the supply of slaves for the Spirit Congregation no doubt, but would still not solve the guardian angel shortage. Yet another debate rages on in the Spirit Congregation whether to change human suicide status from mortal to venial sin.

The venial sin option would allow humans to do a one-year stint in purgatory, and this would definitely increase the guardian angel supply. Another thing to ponder, if humans were to venture out into outer space and their population increased into the trillions, the purgatory population would increase to the point where there might not be any more guardian angel shortages . . . unless of course humans become physically immortal like Regintians! As to what the policies would be then, that quandary will be decided only when it happens.

As per our treaty with the spirits, we would not interfere with any newly discovered species like humans in any spiritual way. That would be left up to the spirits themselves, but they have occasionally asked us for support.

ENTRY INTO HEAVEN

So then, how does a Regintian get into heaven and under what circumstances does it happen. Physically immortal Regintians, who can now visit heaven and have a look-see, have a choice to make. As a Regintian, one must decide whether to seek entry into heaven or continued immortality in the physical three-dimensional realm.

When a Regintian finally decides to stay in heaven forever, he makes a choice as to what procedure to use to end his life.

Should he wait until someone kills him? - Just think before all these discoveries were made, being killed was traumatic and a great sadness, but now it's just a philosophical position.

Would he commit suicide? - Of course you will be in that purgatory for one year.

Or die of old age? - This is difficult for Regintians since we cured old age a long time ago, but it is definitely applicable to Earthlings.

If you commit suicide -- with the fate of become a guardian angel for that one year -- you will be assigned an avatar. When you enter into that spiritual realm, if your avatar isn't ready, you will proceed to a queue and wait. Not only is there a shortage of guardian angels but there's also a shortage of their 'container' avatars. Why can't God just create new avatars?

The traditional way of thinking for 'pre-multidimensional-heaven' Regintians and present day humans, is that God has absolute power to create everything He desires. The facts are that even in this 'heavenly' environment, the nature of the universe imposes certain restrictions. The spiritual universe is derived from a multi-dimensional physical universe and without getting into an extremely detailed and complex technical explanation, it is difficult to produce avatars at the scale required to meet all of purgatory's demands.

Due to the quantum nature of multi-dimensionalism, avatars degrade over the centuries and therefore have a limited time span. Consequently, deciding to commit suicide is a probability decision -- like an Earth roulette wheel. When you do it, you might enter purgatory immediately and eureka, one year later you're in heaven. Or you could wait in that queue for who knows how long. You trade the certainty of a mortal existence for the uncertainly of the 'right-away vs. who knows how long gamble'.

By the way, this isn't a theory; this is a fact since all you have to do is take the 200 year voyage to heaven and interview any of the administrators there or even God and they will confirm this for you.

MORE ABOUT ANGELS

Rumors abound among Regintians that some of these 'purgatory' guardian angels would rather remain as guardian angels since they actually believe it is a better life than in heaven (less boring in their minds). There have been confirmed cases of angels becoming so attached to their mortals, they longed to stay with them past the one year requirement.

The first people not to require angels are human atheists, then newborn babies. Newborn babies might not need them for a while considering it will be quite a few years before they get access to heaven from a time point of view.

What is a standard angel? A standard angel is different from a guardian angel. Consider a standard angel as a spirit who has 'clerical' duties and works directly for the Spirit Congregation. Any spirit can apply for these clerical duties including recently admitted Regintians and Earthlings. You have to remember what the basic function of an angel is for. It's not just to prevent temptation and to watch out for you, it's also to spy on you for God and then maybe use you to perform the occasional miracle.

THE DEVIL

There is one more entity to discuss and that is the devil. A devil is anyone who is in hell. Some of the misconceptions and legends that have survived eons are that devils go about in their spiritual disguises and entice mortals to misbehave. This simply isn't true. Regintians and humans don't need enticement to be bad, they are simply good at it without any so-called 'inspiration'.

Devils are people that didn't meet the grade when the numbers on their soul spreadsheets were added up and had to go to hell (no cliché intended). Most devils are Regintians that were there before the Treaty was signed. Humans are now the only mortals that are allowed into hell and are rapidly catching up to the existing numbers of Regintian devils.

I am closely monitoring that point in time when humans do catch up and surpass them in population. I will let everyone know when it happens through some means or other.

THE UNIVERSE

This might be a good time to discuss the universe and whether it had a beginning. The universe has many sections (which Earth scientists aren't yet aware of), anyone of which can be influenced by dark energy. The dark energy is actually gravity from the other sections. Depending on what section you're in, the gravity from the other sections pull on it causing it to expand. When other sections' gravity is diminished, it will set up a situation when our section will contract again and its gravity will affect other sections causing them to expand. Each section appears to be expanding and contracting over a thirty billion year cycle.

As to whether the universe had a beginning, I have to admit that this is a unique human only discussion. The idea that the universe had a beginning never existed in our society. At the very beginning of our civilization when we began to worship gods and spirits, no one ever suggested that the universe had a beginning. When we first discovered Earth and observed the evolution of human thought along with the growth of both secular and religious philosophies, the idea of a beginning had always existed. Since humans always saw things 'beginning', their children, objects being made, nations, organizations, ideas, then it was natural to consider the universe as having had a beginning.

We in contrast, have been more conscious of the existence of matter and since we have always seen and been surrounded by it, we never thought of something beginning since matter has always been there and has never begun.

When an object was created or person born, the matter that was there at the beginning, and later if the object changed (as in a life-form throughout its life), has always been around for billions of years. So our tendency is to always think of 'things' as never having a beginning; only 'concepts' and specific arrangements of matter have beginnings. As far as we know, the Spirit Congregation has always said that both God and the universe never had a beginning and always were. Does the spirit universe have any control over matter?

In both Regintian and human folklore, all matter in the physical universe is under the control of God and spirits. Both our races have greatly exaggerated this. In fact, the control that spirits have over matter is largely due to human and Regintian imagination. Spirits have long had the ability to place thoughts, visions, and hallucinations into mortal's cerebral cortexes using their guardian angels and/ or multi-dimensional nanobots.

In essence that is the only real control spirits have had over matter.

REGINTIANS BECOMING HUMAN

I'd like to mention something about the process of becoming human. Under normal conditions, traveling all over your planet (and sometimes through it) to do our research allows us to mingle and get physically close to humans. It is therefore imperative that we have a proper disguise in the form of either a human like android or a human cloned body with our own brain fitted in the head.

Which one we use depends on what the objective is. If we plan to be in a very cold region where there will not be many humans, then we would use the android. If we are going to be very close to humans in the physical sense, then the clone is a better disguise. Sometimes, if humans are too close to the android models and stare at them long enough, they start noticing strange little things about them that are not human-like; that's why we rarely use them around humans.

How do we use our human clones? We surgically remove our brains, place them in a biological interface that will reconnect all of our nerve endings and make them compatible with the nerve endings in the human skull of the clone. It's a relatively simple operation and takes about thirty minutes with an hour of rest and meditation until the human is fully functional. After that, the Regintian will do a few basic exercises for about twenty minutes until he feels his new body is fine-tuned to his brain.

It is now time to say good-bye.

Appleton will take over again, and the nanobots will stay in your brain until you remove your fingers from the book.

WHAT DO WE WANT?

Hello again. It's Appleton.

What do we want? We are a curious people and our fascination with your civilization has lasted for about 50,000 years. I suppose the main characteristic we have is curiosity. It is one of many just as you humans have. You might say that curiosity is as strong an emotion with us as sex is with you humans. That is why we have spent so much time looking for intelligent life all over the galaxy. We were ecstatic when we discovered Earth.

So what do we want? We want to study and watch you, and then have diplomatic relationships with you later on. As far as I'm concerned, now is the time to formally have diplomatic relationships: more on that later. In this next part, I will explain how we discovered Earth.

Just remember to keep your fingers on the book pages, or anywhere around your e-reader, since part of the explanation will be seen in a special section of the museum, and you will need to keep those nanobots flowing.

PART 2: HOW WE DISCOVERED EARTH

Greetings once more.

You are now in part two, and this section will inform you of what we call our greatest achievement, the discovery of Earth. A special wing of the museum has been created for this session. It is far more three dimensional and realistic, but you will have to relax even more to get the full sensation. Some of the visuals will be views of star systems and clusters that are simply inspirational.

Let us begin. Turn 90 degrees until you see a doorway to your left. Please enter, and sit down in that red chair. Take a deep breath and relax. Remember, you are not physically doing this but are pretending to dream it. Here we go.

Hello.

My name is Farlee. I am honored and privileged to be the host that informs you of how your planet was discovered. I am presently in an avatar just like you are, and I currently reside in the Lunar-Base on the moon. It is my understanding that you can't communicate with me so just relax, and let me do the talking.

Marcus is the name of the person who is credited for the discovery of Earth and died about 25,000 years ago. He was in the transportation business delivering everything from raw materials to passengers.

The display screen on the wall will play for you a recording he made from his own records in Reginta. The nanobots currently residing in your brain will do the translating. This effectively allows you to hear Marcus in his original voice while still understanding it in your own language. Oh one more thing, the video

will interject 20th century names to identify significant places. Here we go.

The very first time I observed the 'solar' system from far away, it didn't appear to be anything special. The usual conditions for the existence of normal life weren't there. Since we had never encountered 'intelligent' life before this event, our criteria weren't exactly based on authentic historical records or patterns. It was based on guesswork derived from the usual ideological philosophies that abounded in our culture.

Out of the hundreds of thousands of stars littered throughout those clusters, our explorers usually ignored your solar system: an area noted for having a low probability of advanced life. On this particular occasion, I was traveling in my transport starship with my usual crew towards a small star cluster near your solar system. The Brotherhood had local explorers in that region and required a variety of special equipment. It was a standard delivery for us as far as I was concerned.

Then something freaky happened. My co-pilot told me, "A defect has just occurred in the navigation system; we better jump back into regular space."

"Go ahead and deactivate the drive," I said.

"Do we know where we are?" I asked the android navigator.

"I believe it's a location no one has ever been to before," responded the navigator. "But we are not too far from our transportation corridor."

I ordered the crew to repair the defect quickly, so we could leave this star system as soon as possible.

My partner and co-pilot Rafu, noticed something interesting on the star chart and said, "Hey look, our standard scans show a blue/green planet, probably brimming with life."

"They're not all that rare, so what's the big deal," I said to my co-pilot.

"You just never know, there could be some new discovery there," he said excitedly.

"OK, let's keep an eye on it while the crew checks the navigation system." I figured we could spare another 30 minutes or so to observe it a little longer.

Later, when I was just about to make a dimensional jump to another star system, the android navigator alerted me, "The drive in the rear of the spaceship just exploded." We were experienced voyagers, and this sort of mishap rarely happens. This emergency condition brought my crew into a near panic state as oxygen rapidly leaked out of the spaceship.

"Get all non-essential crewmembers to their container rooms until this emergency is over," I ordered. One crewmember didn't follow that order; he was a new member hired just before this trip. Despite the panic that was everywhere, he lingered about without offering any help.

Notwithstanding the pandemonium, the head engineer called me and complained, "That new guy you hired just before this trip, he's behaving weird. He hasn't gone to his quarters and lingers around keeping an eye on things, and then disappears."

I glanced at the android panel and asked, "What's the current status?"

The Android said, "They're continuing to repair the drive as well as the breach in the ship's outer hull, but we're still leaking oxygen albeit at a lower rate."

At that exact same moment he noticed, "There's a shuttlecraft departing our main vessel."

Not quite panicking yet, I said to Rafu, "Could the person on that shuttle be the one who sabotaged our spaceship and the suspicious new crewmember?"

"I wouldn't bet against it," he said.

"Take the other shuttle and go after that guy while we 'park' our spaceship on that tiny blue green planet. It has a rich supply of oxygen and we're going to grab some of it."

While waiting for my partner to return, we carefully scrutinized everything on board our spaceship. The head engineer blurted, "We found another destructive device *planted near the hyperspace drive that could completely destroy our spaceship."*

"Can we disable it in time?"

The android controller interjected, "That device will explode in another 5 minutes. I think you better make plans to abandon ship."

Apparently, the person who escaped had also damaged several important sensors preventing us from monitoring everything on the ship, and that more or less ended our attempt to save it.

I radioed my partner just before he got too far away, "Rafu, stop the chase and get your butt back to the ship; we have to evacuate it."

The hyperspace drive finally exploded causing us to fall out of Earth orbit towards the planet. A crash was unavoidable, so we evacuated the spaceship using both my partner's shuttlecraft and an extra one we had on board. The doomed spaceship eventually crash-landed and created a huge crater.

This is Farlee again, sorry for this interjection.

The location the spaceship crash-landed in was the state of Arizona in the United States. If you think this is the 'Arizona Crater' then you are correct. Please note that you will not find any residue of a technological or unusual alien nature in that crater. That type of thing was removed a long time ago just in case humans became knowledgeable enough to analyze it and determine its non-earthly origins.

Back to Marcus.

The two shuttles landed near the massive crater that our ship had inadvertently created. Normally, we'd begin to look for ways to leave this world, but we were simply agog at all the life surrounding us. It was inspiring.

Fortunately, our communications equipment was functioning at a normal level in these two shuttles, and we were able to send an emergency signal back to the local shipping corridors near this star cluster. In the meantime, we had no idea what happened to that escaped shuttle my partner had stopped chasing.

So we settled down and after three years of waiting, a large spaceship came to the rescue. During that waiting period however, we 'flipped' when we discovered human beings. Yes, they were uneducated hunter-gatherers living in Africa, but they did have a great intelligence that only us in this galaxy (at least in the part we have explored) had possessed so far.

We proceeded back to our home world and in 400 years were back with an expedition of three large exploration cruisers. That was exactly 49,282 years ago, and I had the privilege of leading one of them.

During our discussions of how to explore Earth, we contemplated whether we should communicate with Earthlings: should we educate them to comprehend the universe, or encourage them to move towards a more civilized society.

We didn't have any difficulty believing humans could gain this knowledge since they certainly had the intellectual ability to acquire and retain it.

There were several issues to resolve though. The first was, do we have the right to alter their normal evolutionary process? Would humans stay hunter gathers without our support, or would they gradually learn about the nature of matter and the universe by themselves?

The second issue was to find out what they would do without our involvement. Would they become as sophisticated as we are for example?

Arguments against this second issue were that we shouldn't be exploiting the usual human civilization process just for our own curiosity about how they would proceed under normal conditions. This debate continued for a while with the 'leaving them alone' viewpoint winning out.

The next step was to set up Monitoring Stations around the globe to study Earth's nature and in Africa to monitor human development without interrupting human activity.

It was obvious that after one year of study, we would have to wait a long time before humans improved in an evolutionary way, so we decided to come back every thousand years or so to monitor their progress.

It's Farlee again.

Well by now, we know that you did. You are beginning to travel in outer space and have begun to unravel the mysteries of the universe even though I must admit, sometimes we did have to help out a bit. We will be discussing this later during your stay here.

Before we go back to Marcus, Appleton is indicating to me that a member of the Spirit Congregation is ready for his meeting with you. When they heard about the publication of this book, they insisted on meeting every human that visits here. The greeting you are about to encounter is the usual way a spirit member expects to meet with humans. It is in the form of a prayer and I must warn you that it goes on for a long time. We have to go into this room next to the video display, and we'll just stand near the door. Here he comes and he will begin praying in the manner of the culture you have been raised in.

OH GREAT FATHER LIVING IN HEAVEN, THOU NAME IS THE MOST HOLIEST AND THY KINGDOM IS THE GREATEST AND

THOU SHALT HAVE THE GREATEST INFLUENCE IN THE UNIVERSE.
THOU HAST ONLY TO DISPENSE THY ENTITIES WITH THY PRAYERS AND HOLINESS AND ALL WILL BE FORGIVEN.

Pssst, human. What you're hearing will go on for hours. We don't exactly know how long because we've never stayed around long enough to find out.

THY SPIRIT IS THE MOST HOLIEST, MOST GRACIOUS AND MOST HONORABLE.

One thing we have noticed is that this entity is so engrossed in prayer, he can't hear us if we speak softly enough and once he gets going, isn't really aware of us, so let's walk quietly out of the room and close this door . . .

OH GREAT LORD, THOU MUST FORGIVE OUR SINS...

... that's better.

Before we waste any more time let's get back to the Marcus video and listen to his chronicle on the beginning of the civilizational process for humans.

WATCHING CIVILIZATION GROW

After five of these trips, totaling 5,000 years, we saw little improvement in human's technological advancement except for one thing.

OUT OF AFRICA

When we returned on that fifth trip, we notice certain areas covered by desert in Africa had expanded and observed that some pockets of humans, who had stayed in certain forested and plains area, were surrounded by desert. This wasn't so bad except for the fact that the desert part was continuing to grow. It was going to be a disaster for thousands of humans, so we decided to interfere on an emergency basis.

Altering weather patterns in areas that were going to become deserts was the method we used to ensure they would stay rich in vegetation. The desert expansion delay allowed them time to access the East of Africa, then cross into what you called the Middle East, and then branch out into Europe and Asia. All this effort was insurance to make sure the human species would not go extinct.

It worked.

The continents of Europe and Asia later became populated with humans. We justified this action by believing humans would have done it anyway, only maybe a few thousand years later with far fewer humans and more risk.

Later, more exits out of Africa happened without our interference and humans expanded all over the world.

It's Farlee again.

There was a bit more evolution on your part, and we don't mean your skin color changing or anything like that. Some of your species actually branched off in certain isolated areas of the world and changed quite a bit. Humans in the 20th century later discovered fossils of these species, which includes 'Red Deer people' found in China between 1979 and 2012, and 'Flores Man' found in Indonesia in 2002. Back to Marcus.

As time went on, extra Monitoring Stations were placed in out-of-the-way areas making our observations more productive. These Stations were supposed to be kept a secret so human development would not be disturbed. We were still determined to have a hands-off policy despite our 'out of Africa' intervention and the fact that the Stations were never disguised. Unfortunately, things happen that are sometimes beyond our control in spite of our confidence humans would not ever see them.

So it was a surprise to us when one of our Stations was discovered by several roving humans one day. Later, we found out they had some guidance. Remember that person who stole the shuttle from my spaceship a few hundred years ago and tried to sabotage our voyage, he was actually leading these people to find us in these remote areas. He had been living on Earth all these years. We found him out of sheer chance when we scanned a group of humans who were destroying a Station they had taken over. The scan indicated they were calling the Station the home of the devil.

What would encourage these natives to believe it was an evil place as opposed to a holy one? One of them caught our attention. His behavior was slightly different, and it was obvious he had more intelligence than the rest of them.

One of our stealthy shuttlecraft was sent down during the night to hover over this person and his followers when they slept, and discovered a slight difference in his physiology compared with the rest of his group. His DNA was different and definitely not related to any of the other humans.

The investigation continued by sending in a swarm of nanobots that could penetrate his body and get a more detailed scan of what was going on. We were startled at the result. What we discovered was that he was the missing Regintian who had sabotaged our spaceship and hijacked a shuttlecraft. He was a human clone with a Regintian brain; similar to the clones we use when we explore Earth on foot. How did he get his hands on a human clone since they had not yet been developed at the time we discovered Earth?

When the nanobot analysis was done it was determined this person was an authentic Regintian who had allowed a spirit, or angel -- or whatever, to infiltrate his mind. He had disguised himself as one of our crewmembers when this mind infiltration happened all those years ago. The Congregation had colluded with this person and kept him alive and healthy during this long period of time on Earth before he was rediscovered by us.

Why did the Spirit Congregation do all of these things?

Since we had signed that treaty of 'Spiritual Truth' eons ago, we thought every issue had been put to rest. The Spirit Congregation had always been a very secretive organization, and for many thousands of years we assumed they knew all the major life forms that existed around the galaxy and possibly the universe.

It took us a long time to find out, but this so-called established fact simply wasn't true. They had no knowledge of other intelligent beings in the galaxy similar to humans, so for many thousands of years they planted spirits/angels on our ships waiting to find out if we would ever discover them.

The facts were that with Regintians now living extremely long lives, the amount of entries into heaven was way down, and discovering a new intelligent species would bring those numbers back up in the long run.

That's why our ship was sabotaged. The saboteur wanted to inform the Congregation about this major discovery and at the same time prevent the Regintian Brotherhood from knowing about it. Obviously it didn't work, so he hid on Earth all these years studying what we were doing and reporting it to the Congregation.

The purpose of this intrigue was to make sure the second intelligent species in the galaxy would worship the Congregation in the way they desired, not the half-baked attempt that our species had with our 'Spiritual Treaty' etc.

For the most part, there was an overwhelming inconsistency in this whole approach of 'information gathering'. The Spirit Congregation usually had no problems in acquiring all of our expedition knowledge because they already had numerous guardian angels in a variety of explorers presently on Earth. So they should be up-to-date on all discoveries taking place. It didn't seem logical to us to even bother using a spy. Then again, logic never was an 'attribute' of the Spirit Congregation.

Once we had all the data sent back to Reginta, we confronted the spirit world yet again. The Brotherhood immediately requested a meeting with God and 'politely' demanded to know what the 'hell' was going on. To be quite honest with you, the Brotherhood wasn't expecting an immediate response from God and assumed they would have to deal with some lower intermediaries.

However, God surprised them by scheduling a meeting in heaven right away and stating:

"I would wholeheartedly like to apologize for what happened in the Solar System. Yes, I was aware we had one of our angels on your ship, but realize that the crewmember, who had the angel take over his body, had volunteered to do so. There is nothing in the Treaty of Spiritual Truth to state he can't. What shouldn't have happened was for him to attempt the destruction of not only your ship but also its crewmembers, as well as keeping the discovery of Earth a secret. This particular angel is too much of a zealot, and I promise you he will be punished. Again, I sincerely apologize and promise this won't happen again as our angels will now undergo a improved vetting process before they are assigned duties in the mortal world."

As the meeting continued, a deal was worked out. Since humans would probably end up worshiping *something anyway, they might as well worship the Spirits in the Congregation. Why should we care? What the Congregation coveted was the exclusive 'human deference' of being worshiped. Humans of course could have worshiped either God or us since Regintians were so scientifically advanced, we would appear like gods to them. But since the Congregation were the real spirits, we might as well let them take all the religious credit. We didn't care to be worshiped since our egos didn't extend that far into the hinterland of narcissism.*

How could they get humans to focus on the Congregation only? The method would be to allow the odd 'miracle' to take place, thus confirming in human eyes the actuality of the spirit world and existence of God/gods. Here's an example of what I mean.

If humans inadvertently bumped into us and saw our strange technology by accident, we wouldn't claim credit for miracles or other spiritual phenomenon. We would allow the Spirits to handle these inadvertent encounters in whatever way that would allow humans to direct their worship at them and not us.

I have to admit there were times when we would roll our eyes in our head (to use a human phrase here) and be amazed at the incredible ego gratification seeking mentality of the Spirit Congregation. By that famous treaty of ours, we did not have to worship them to go to heaven, and their actions on Earth were certainly not enticing any of us to adapt that attitude.

Hello, Farlee again: this brings to a close Marcus' narration of his transcripts.

One thing that wasn't clearly explained was how did that spy obtain a human form while on Earth. An investigation revealed that he spent the first years of his life in his original Regintian form and when we finally developed our human cloning capability, he had a collaborator send one down for his own use.

Let me expand further on the relationship between humans and the Congregation. The following is an example of the gradual 'alignment' of human spiritual focus towards the Congregation.

ALTAMIRA

Something happen around 30,000 years ago, and we're still not sure what effect it had on human development. Remember the drawings at Altamira in the caves in Spain. Most humans have at one time read about or studied them in school. One of our people actually began these paintings by mistake. I am naming this person Potpaint since as usual his identification is unpronounceable in earth-speak.

Potpaint had cloned himself a human body in the usual manner, so he could explore cave dwellings near an area referred to as Altamira in Spain. He waited until the occupants had left to go hunting and then sneaked in to take pictures and obtain chemical samples. Unfortunately, he had no navigation aids available when he ventured into this intricate cave for the first time. That was a very foolish thing to have done.

It wasn't too long before he became lost and by the time he had figured a way out, it was too late; the humans had arrived. He had no desire to be their prisoner in case they became violent and felt defenseless since he never expected to be stuck there.

Out of desperation, he came up with a brilliant idea to make a drawing of an animal he knew these people hunted, and maybe, just maybe, they would be so impressed, he would be able to leave if this painting distracted them enough. At worse, they might consider him a spirit and still let him go, so maybe this strategy would work.

It worked so well, Potpaint sneaked out as they all stood there in awe of the painting. Talk about inspiration; next thing you know they began doing their own paintings, which eventually became a habit, and then a love, right up until present times. I am not stating that without us they wouldn't have started this themselves, but let's face it, that error did inspire these first paintings.

MIGRATION TO THE AMERICAS

After the experience of mistakenly exposing ourselves to humans and the way the Spirit Congregation exploited these mistakes for their own religious gratification, a decision was made to be more careful about where we placed our Stations on Earth. Someone took the initiative of placing them as far north as possible since humans at the time hadn't really tolerated these cold weather climates.

That plan went well for a few thousand years or so until the incident of the Great Barrier Reef in Alaska. Our expedition fleet was using that reef as a landing place for our large cruisers, as well as a base Station. At the time, we weren't paying too much attention to natural erosions in the area, but certain parts of it were constantly flooding, which was a nuisance. The solution was to place rock formations in key areas to prevent this flooding and stabilize the landing area.

Next thing you know, humans discovered these pathways. That put an end to the use of those landing areas over the long haul and within a few hundred years, the expedition fleet had to relocated to new ones. The humans eventually found their way into North America utilizing these abandoned pathways. Of course, since we stopped using these areas, the land formations gradually eroded away and went back to normal.

By then it was too late, North America, and later South America, now had become populated with humans. Was this inadvertent interference good or bad? There was an additional thing to consider.

At the very beginning, the trip from that passageway towards the south was very treacherous and difficult to pass as well as extremely cold. Our large space cruisers had to occasionally hold back glaciers, rivers, and landslides. Since this mess was caused by us to being with, humans shouldn't be held responsible for these natural hardships, so we did help them out a little bit.

The Congregation took advantage of our support by encouraging beliefs in miracles, which would confirm the existence of the spiritual world. I have to admit, their attitude upset us. We thought they should perform their own 'real' miracles rather than exploiting our good work. Their attitude was: "What difference does it make as long as they worship us." Well the difference should be a question of honesty don't you think. I mean if you seek to promote honesty, please do not exploit our good deeds as something that has to do you with your alleged abilities. It was as if history was repeated itself.

The 'Treaty of Spiritual Truth' set out to state exactly what was good and bad and in what context. Obviously, the Congregation was treating humans with the old pre-treaty conceptions. The usual pre-treaty stuff like: if God says it's good then it's good, and if He says it's bad then it's bad.

Our exploration staff -- not being the religiously deferential types -- shook their heads in disgust every time the Congregation exploited the good things we did to humans for their own gratification. However, here is an incident that the Congregation had nothing to do with, and we must take full responsibility.

HUMANS ESTABLISHING ROOTS

STONEHENGE

This, you might say is the beginning of one of the most unusual events in the early epochs of human civilization. Just before the time Stonehenge was built, the British Isles were sparsely inhabited compared with today. It was one of the places we occasionally flew over, not as interesting as Egypt or Mesopotamia, but interesting enough to realize that social and intelligent humans were all over the world. We acquired the habit of landing our spacecraft just about anywhere since most of the time humans were not present.

The following is an account from the captain of a shuttle that flew over the area in the British Isles known as Stonehenge.

One day, about 3,100 Earth years ago, we had a few technical problems and searched for a deserted place to land on. When our ship landed, someone noticed that our hyperspace drive propulsion unit wasn't functioning properly, so our repair service came down to fix it. So far, no one on our spaceship noticed any humans, making it an ideal place to land.

When the repair craft arrived, it had become quite foggy and since this craft had rapidly descended from outer space, it had a high temperature on one side caused by air friction as it was coming in. Under normal conditions, as soon as a craft like this enters the atmosphere, the temperature on the under-body stabilizes quickly and reaches the same temperature as the air.

On this occasion, the pilot thought the repair mission was an emergency and descended much faster than normal. Our crafts are capable of descending quickly; it's not like the American space shuttle, which takes time. We can be 120 miles above the Earth's surface and down to sea level within seconds. So this was the speed the pilot chose when coming to our 'rescue'.

This caused the outside temperature on the craft's hull to reach levels that affected the moisture distribution in the atmosphere just above our spaceship -- which was now situated in the middle of a field.

What would a person standing outside in that field see? More than likely, a glowing haze and cloud structure emanating from the sky.

What if that person was a human with no scientific understanding and witnessed these events? Would he consider this a religious experience? If you thought yes, then you would be right.

It just so happened that a few kilometers away out of sight of our ship, there were farmers tolling in the field. The brightness they saw in the sky didn't go unnoticed. They consulted their leadership and sent a small party out in the direction of our ship. One of the people in that party was a religious leader, go figure. I remember one of my crewmembers, who was monitoring outside the ship through a special viewer for anything unusual, saying, "Oh oh".

I looked outside, and there in the distance were six people strolling towards our ship with frighten gazes on their faces. There was still a lot of fog outside, and one can imagine as they approached the ship what an imposing structure its appearance must have been.

In contrast, I felt like I had been caught doing something mischievous, what to do now? The best thing to do would be to leave right away and become another legend of which there were many among these people, and ours would just fade away into history. Since the repair craft was on top doing the repair work, it wouldn't be ready to take off for another day!

So what happened? The humans came to within 500 meters of our ship, knelt down, and appeared to pray. At least that's what it sounded like when we heard the chanting. Next thing you know, three of them left, and the three that stayed behind lied down flat on their bellies in what appeared to be a worshipful pose. Our attitude? Oh shit, what have we done now?

Two hours later, a new group of twenty people appeared. Several of these people were carrying carved symbols, some had large sheets of cloth, and others had strange symbols in their possession.

Next thing you know, they spread out in a circle surrounding our ship (which has a circular shape by the way), and they all get down on their knees. Out in the distance we notice a single individual with a pen and parchment in hand writing something down. The flight engineer sent over a flying probe containing a camera to see what he was doing. As it got there, it sent back a video of him drawing a picture of our ship. It didn't look good for our policy of non-interference.

The next day, after the repair ship finished their work, we decided to play a few tricks. An artificial fog was created that was so dense, the people surrounding the ship would not be able to see it even at that distance. When the ship rose vertically, it was so slow they could hear nothing at all.

Next, our flight engineer lifted the fog by remote control so they would see absolutely nothing after it had dissipated. Despite our careful plans, we did forget about one tiny little thing. The ground still had our imprint on it. Would they notice this and seek inspiration from it? Don't bet against it.

In the next few years structures of wood appeared, and eventually the place became what you humans call Stonehenge. The farming community continued to build and adjust these structures during the next thousand years. Later, stone structures began to appear and evolve until the majority of them were finished around 2,000 B.C.: all because of our little repair job.

Excuse me for a moment. I'm getting a signal from Appleton . . . Yes?

Thank you Farlee.

I hoped you found that little exposition enjoyable. It certainly enlightens ancient Earth history, does it not?

Next, Farlee is going to guide you to that part of history referred to as the agricultural phase of your civilization. But before he does that, would you like a drink. You might be wondering how an Avatar can drink. Simple, we have special Avatar liquids designed specifically for Avatar entities. They make you think you are refreshed even though your human body back on Earth will not physically feel anything. They are completely free of charge (the costs are actually calculated into the price of this book you're reading), and you can have as many as you like.

There is only one little problem. You have to verbally communicate with us that you desire a drink; otherwise, we are not in the position where we can legally give them to you.

Farlee, has this human said anything to you since you've met him?

No he hasn't, but I can tell from his body language that he is definitely paying attention to everything the narrators and I have said.

Human, Go ahead and say something. It has to be an audible communication and not sign language . . . .

Looks like this one still can't speak Farlee. You might as well continue with your discussion.

I have several more events to tell you about. These are summaries of what happened, so I won't be getting into a huge amount of detail. That will be for later when we fully reveal ourselves in your societies.

This information is a compilation of the explorer's documentation of those days. Even though we are physically immortal, none of those people are alive today. Accidents, killings and suicides can happen over 5,000 years.

EGYPTIAN PYRAMIDS

We had nothing to do with the Egyptian pyramids, contrary to many controversial theories written by speculative Earth historians. They did attract a lot of attention from us since they were much bigger than previous structures created by humans.

They were such interesting edifices that we set up both a stationary observation platform hovering just above Egypt in outer space and an Earth based station disguised as a simple home in the Egyptian capital. The home was used when we required close observation of what was going on. Everything proceeded smoothly for the first hundred years until some soldiers or criminals (under certain rulers you couldn't tell the difference) decided to loot our home. This quickly became an emergency once they had stolen the special 3D projection equipment hidden there. If you pressed certain controls on this equipment, it could project a large variety of realistic images. Something unexpected might happen to human progress since the technology was so beyond them at the time, we were sure it would have a major influence.

The explorer who was living in this home was named Massachucets. I will let his great-great-great-grandson, Evilochets tell you more about what happened.

Ok Evilo, go ahead.

Greetings Earthling.

I am going to read from Massachucets' diary, and I'm sure you'll be fascinated by the way he became a close friend to an important human in Egyptian history. Here is the story just at the point when he discovered the equipment had been looted from his home:

They took my damn equipment away and hid it. It took a few days, but I eventually found it in a building where they kept their 'god-forsaken' religious objects. I wasn't too surprised when they stored it in that little 'temple' since this 'toy' of mine sometimes lit up. That certainly would have led them to consider its worthiness for placing it there since they have never seen this type of object before.

I deployed a special eavesdropping probe and found where it was. The area they brought it to was a holding place for items waiting to be placed inside a pyramid once the ruler was buried there. Apparently, they considered this a spiritual object (what else!).

The name of the Egyptian controlling this was Imhotep who later became a revered figure in Egyptian history. I think I might have had something to do with his fame.

Nevertheless, during this period, Imhotep was a very young man with no particular influence among the rulers of Egypt other than being born into the upper classes. When I first met him, he had already seen the 3D projection and automatically assumed it was from a god or had spiritual significance. It wasn't easy meeting with him since he was so well protected by an entourage of bodyguards.

But I had my ways and was able to control the guards surrounding his little headquarters by making them fall asleep with a non-toxic gas. Then it was a simple matter of walking in, albeit very quietly, until I spotted a young authoritative figure relaxing in a grand-looking chair with his feet up on what could be an altar.

When I entered his domain, he looked confused and assumed I was just a servant he had never seen before.

"Who are you and what are you doing in this sacred room?" he said.

"Sacred?" I said, "You don't look so sacred to me using that altar as a pedestal for your feet."

He seemed startled by my high-handed way. Servants do not talk to the upper classes in such a manner.

"How dare you speak to me like that. Who let you into this room?"

"I am here to retrieve my personal property that was stolen by your servants."

"What thing are you talking about?"

With the remote control device in my possession, it wasn't too difficult to activate the 3D projector, which was leaning against the wall. The 3D image that projected from the unit was a simulation of a god they worshipped. I was hoping that members of the Spirit Congregation who might be observing this session with Imhotep would realize this projection was to their benefit since it would simply reinforce his belief in their religion. When he saw this figure, he automatically assumed I was part of this deity and became totally paralyzed with fear.

"Don't worry. Have no fear; you will not be harmed in any way. My friend," I was pointing to that projection, "wants me to take him away from here and go back to where he was living."

I heard a slamming noise just outside the room we were in and knew there were other guards closing all the doors leading to the outside. It seems not everyone was asleep when I entered the building, and these people might have been reacting to secret signals from Imhotep.

A very frighten person with a weapon burst into the room. Imhotep said, "It's OK. Leave us alone. I will be fine." The guard left.

Suddenly, I found myself stuck inside this building, since the guards had closed the entrance, with no method of escape. As we continued our discussion, Imhotep told me take him to the spirit world, which in his mind would mean killing both of us. Sorry, but I wasn't ready to kill myself. Even though there was no pathway to hell for me, I certainly wasn't ready for that one-year stint in purgatory as a guardian angel.

"Imhotep, it isn't done this way. If you desire to live well in the afterlife, the way to do it is by achieving great accomplishments."

For someone who was scared as hell just a few minutes ago, he seemed to have a lot of gall attempting to negotiate with me his passageway into the afterlife.

"How do I know you are not the devil who is trying to steal this sacred object?"

"A real devil would have killed you immediately and already brought you to hell."

He didn't seem to be anymore deferential towards an angel type figure or a devilish one. As this little chitchat went back and forth, he finally agreed to let me go but insisted on keeping the device. That was simply not acceptable, so I had to come up with a plan.

"Give me that object", I said pointing to the device, "and I will bestow on you extraordinary powers that will allow you to achieve great deeds in your lifetime."

That was a lie of course. I was relying on the fact that because he thought of me as a deity of sorts, he would believe me and let me go. The negotiations continued for a while, so I ended up creating a contraption out of the case that held the projection unit but removing the technology. The only thing he acquired was the shell of the device with none of the equipment.

Incidentally, this shell is now in a museum in Egypt, and its reputation as having been influence by beings from outer space is considered a myth!

Let me clear up another little mystery for you human historians. Imhotep's tomb has never been found, and the reason for this is that he is the only human to have ever been removed from Earth and brought to our world.

That is an interesting story. I kept in touch with Imhotep just to see how Egyptian civilization was developing under his influence and to observe whether the Spirit Congregation might be manipulating his society. I didn't notice anything from them that could be called unscrupulous. They weren't revealing any advanced technology or knowledge and were encouraging the Egyptians to continue worshiping their deities.

Over the years, I became fairly good friends with Imhotep and did start feeling sorry for him as he approached death in his old age. Occasionally, the Regintian exploration management needs to contact the Spirit Congregation. Through this procedure, I managed to find out that they were not considering him for entry into heaven.

That was strange, so I asked them why. Their response was that Imhotep didn't worship them sufficiently, and this might have an influence on other humans if he arrived in heaven causing a reduction in their worshiping. I was flabbergasted and asked them what difference it made if some humans reduced their deference a bit. After all, we Regintians don't have to worship them, so why would a slightly less worshipful attitude by a few humans make a difference?

They told me they were concerned this influence could spread. That was the last time I bothered trying to communicate with these ego driven idiots, so I decided to sneak Imhotep back to Reginta. There was one little difficulty however. The Brotherhood was definitely against bringing any human to Reginta and their policy was rigid.

I ignored this rule and secretly brought him home. He died about one hundred years later. His life could have extended for the longest time, but he was insistent on not living forever. I let him have his wish.

And that is the part of the diary of my great great great grandfather Massachucets.

Thank you Evilochets. Appleton?

NOAH

This is Appleton again.

I'm predicting most Earthlings will not like the way this next section is written. The best way to describe the methodology of the following pages is to use that time worn cliché, 'Lawyers nightmare'. There are two versions of Noah's Ark presented in this book. The first one is a believer's version: a believer in the context of being a Spirit Congregation follower, which means all religions on Earth. If viewing or reading this version, be aware that the Spirit Congregation has attached a Certificate of Authenticity.

The second one is the Regintian version from our own records. There is one little problem. The Spirit Congregation refuses to allow anyone who reads their version to read anyone else's. This means that you, the reader of this book, cannot read the Regintian version, which comes right after the believer's version. The Spirit Congregation has insisted that you swear an oath to this effect.

The procedure for taking the oath is as follows: place your thumb in the square provided allowing the nanobots to sense its presence, and your oath will be registered with the Spirit Congregation.

You might or might not have a guardian angel presently residing in your soul. It depends on current shortages. If you do, then the reading of the Regintian version, after swearing this oath, will be marked on your soul spreadsheet as a grave mortal sin and I, Appleton, will not be responsible for any consequences that might result.

Here is the oath. You must read it aloud and place your thumb in the square.

The account of the flooding incidents being summarized here is a revelation to me, a certified human being.

I hereby swear that I believe this is the absolute truth, the whole truth, and nothing but the truth, so help me Spirit Congregation.

I acknowledge there will be no lies or untruths in the telling of this version.

I also acknowledge that it is sent to me directly from heaven, so it is the very latest version of God's will with unbridled accuracy.

I have placed my thumb in the square and swear that I will not read any other version, so help me Spirit Congregation.

Most versions of this flood, while attempting to be as honest as possible, are not necessarily accurate. For example, there are discrepancies among the Christian, Muslim, and Jewish versions. There is also the Gnostic, Baha'i faith, and Mesopotamian versions, along with others.

This is not because of an attempt by these cultures to fool or lie to people. It's simply the ability of humans to allow indulging in the narration process based on centuries old practices. The three main versions are as honestly recorded as possible and to be quite candid with you, the differences are trivial. The Christian version had a huge ark, all of Earth's species, only 8 family members on board, a worldwide flood, with the ark finally resting on Mount Ararat, while the Muslim version had a flat watercraft composed of logs, Noah's domestic animals only, 76 people on board, a local flood only, and final resting place on Mount Judi.

The following is the official certified version based on the Spirit Congregation's records. It is certified to be 100% accurate and true containing no cultural biases or political ambitions of any kind. If the present reader has any other versions of the flood from the Spirit Congregation, we will refund the money you spent on this book. Just send the 'Alleged True Version' of the story along with your book receipt to:

Noah Flood Narrative Dept.
Reginta Brotherhood.
Planet Reginta
Omega Centauri Globular cluster
Milky Way galaxy.

You can either send this by regular mail (it will take 400 years to get there) or email it to MassageDeMessuer@OmegaCentauriGlobularCluster.MK Galaxy.

Please be patience as this star cluster is approximately 16,000 light years away, it can take a few hundred years before you get an answer even when sending it by hyper-quad-dimensional com-stream communications.

Because our contract with the hyper-quad-dimensional com-stream communications company is presently under negotiation for renewal, we cannot use the real-time method that is normally use when visitors like you come to Reginta.

[SG] 1011 0111

[0001] Through the wondrous and magnificent management of the Lord, man became more wicked. The Great Lord had hopeth that when men were discovered 51,238 Earth years ago they wouldith becometh good and holy. The Great Lord becamith sad and disappointed. And the LORD said, I willith destroyth man whom I have createdith from the face of the Earth; both man, and beast, and the creeping thing, and the fowls of the air; for it repenteth me that I have madeth them. He gaveth the order to the Spirit Congregation to destroyth men and all beasts and animals and creeping things.

[0010] But the Spirit Congregation pointed out rightfully that Noah and members of his family were good and constantly worshipping the Great Lord and praising him. The Great Lord was grateful for this information and gaveth the order to destroyth everything but Noah and his family.

[0011] But the Spirit Congregation pointed out rightfully that the Orientals, the Indians, the Africans, and the American and Australian aboriginals were not as bad. They prayed more, worshipped more, believed in miracles more, and committed less sins. The Great Lord was grateful for this information and gaveth the order to destroy men and living things only in the Middle East.

[0100] But the Spirit Congregation pointed out rightfully that animals and beasts and creeping things were incapable of sinning since they behaved just as the Lord hath created them. The Great Lord was again grateful for this information and then said unto Noah, thou art a good person Noah, build me a large boat to carry many animals.

[0101] Make thee an ark of gopher wood; rooms shalt thou make in the ark, and shalt pitch it within and without with pitch. And this is the fashion which thou shalt make it of: The length of the ark shall be three hundred cubits, the breadth of it fifty cubits, and the height of it thirty cubits. And Noah starteth to built a great boat to carrieth all the animals of the world. And of every living thing of all flesh, two of every sort shalt thou bringth into the ark, to keep them alive with thee; they shall be male and female. Of fowls after their kind, and of cattle after their kind, of every creeping thing of the earth after his kind, two of every sort shall come unto thee, to keep them alive.

[0110] But the Spirit Congregation pointed out rightfully that animal species were in thy millions as a result of thy evolution created by thou, oh Great Lord. Thy ark wilt not carrieth all thy animal species.

The Great Lord was again grateful for this information and then reinstructed Noah, thou shalt use his own domesticated animals.

[0111] But the Spirit Congregation pointed out rightfully that the ark was now way too big to carry only Noah's domesticated animals.

The Great Lord was again grateful for this information and then reinstructed Noah to make thee an ark in the following manner.

Thou shalt make Noah's ark as a flat watercraft made of logs, tied together with ropes.

[1000] For the next seven days I will cause it to rain upon thy Earth forty days and forty nights; and every living substance that I have made will I destroy from off the face of the Earth. And the waters prevailed upon the Earth a hundred and fifty days.

[1001] But the Spirit Congregation pointed out rightfully that thou flood was local, around thy Dead Sea area only.

The Great Lord was again grateful for this information and reinstructed Noah that thou rains wilt last four days and a minor flood wilt last only 15 days around thy Dead Sea area only. And thy ark rested in thy first month, on thy seventeenth day of thy month, half on upon mount Ararat and half upon mount Judi.

[**1010**] But thy Spirit Congregation pointed out rightfully that since thou flood was local around thy Dead Sea area only then thy ark wilt not haveth traveled far upon thy mountains of Ararat let alone splitting up in half.
The Great Lord was again grateful for this information and then reinstructed Noah to not to worry about landing in a strange place.

[**1011**] The Lord said in his heart, I will not again curse the ground anymore for man's sake; for the imagination of man's heart is evil from his youth; neither will I again smite any more everything living, as I have done because I shalt not ever go through this nightmare of decision making again. And the Spirit Congregation praisith the Lord his reasonable and brilliant upgrades to his temper.

[**1100**] And Noah planted a vineyard: And he drank of the wine, and was drunken; and he was uncovered within his tent. And Ham, the father of his son Canaan, saw the nakedness of his father and did nothing to hide the nakedness, but told his two brethren. And Shem and Japheth took a garment, and laid it upon both their shoulders, and went backward so they would not see their father's nakedness, and covered his nakedness; And Noah awoke from his wine, and knew what his younger son Ham had done unto him. And he said, Cursed be the son of Ham, Canaan; he shall be a servant of servants unto his brethren. And he said, Blessed be the Lord God of Shem; and Canaan the son of Ham shall be his servant.

[**1101**] But the Spirit Congregation pointed out rightfully to Noah that in no way was Canaan, the son of Ham, responsible for the wrongs of his father.
The Great Lord again agreed with this rational insight into the basic rights of human beings and instructed Noah not to make Canaan a servant.

[**1110**] And Noah lived after the flood three hundred and fifty years. And all the days of Noah were 950 years: and he died.

[**1111**] But the Spirit Congregation pointed out rightfully that Noah lived 950 months which is 79 years and not 950 years.

The Great Lord again agreed with this rational calculation and congratulated the Spirit Congregation on their ability to do basic arithmetic.

He was further i pres ed.... . . . .

.

.

[1xxxx > exception error: Permission denied to call Congregation Server]

<Spirit script unable to understand windows 8 update>

Brotherhood notification #23def58-Unfortunately we have to end this section since out of admiration for Earth's innovative computer technology in the 20th and 21st centuries (which is inferior to ours) we attempted to use binary notation to keep track of these verses but unfortunately the field we used to number it was only 4 bits wide and overflowed, causing our stream of data to crash.

Since this book was to be published the following day, we did not have enough time to reformat that section and had to submit it as is.

Sorry.

=========================

REGINTIAN VERSION

If up until now you have been a very religious person, especially a follower of an Abrahamic religion, you will have a lot of trouble believing this version of events. This is why the Spirit Congregation made you swear an oath.

But we did warn you, and if you've decided not to read their version then here is ours.

Sometime around 4,000 years ago, a large group of scientists graduated from our Earth studies university, and all of them yearned to travel to Earth as a group. Unfortunately, there wasn't enough room in our standard size space cruiser. Under normal circumstances, we have anywhere from 150 to 200 explorers on Earth and the Lunar-Base, and another 50 for various explorative assignments in the solar system. Earth studies had become so popular that our educational system produced far more graduates than what was required. This particular year one of the graduating students, who was a member of the Regintian brotherhood, came up with a bright idea.

Why not initiate a special project that would use at least another 200 Regintians. This project still wouldn't provide enough work for the much larger amount of graduates the school produced, but it was better than nothing. The Brotherhood Council discussed the matter, approved it, and a special ship was even designed and built for the occasion. Most of these graduates were from wealthy and influential backgrounds, so this 'ark' (which was more like a luxury cruise liner) became a unique 'class symbol' for these people.

One of the features this ship was designed with was the capacity to hold all types of Earth animal species from all over the world in special housings and cages. One incredible feature it had was the ability to float and go underwater in the deepest of oceans. The advantage of this capability was the magnificent view it would have of marine life, which would make it easy to select marine species.

It took a year to build and the usual 150 years to travel to Earth. During that period, it was obvious to anyone on the ship that these recent 'graduates' were in party mode most of the time. Regintians do not party like humans. There's no cheering or laughter but that doesn't mean there isn't any enjoyment. Things can get out of hand and become wild like in a human party. Our wildness usually results in violence against physical objects with none against each other, but we do enjoy breaking things.

There was one little problem this time. Great care was taken in designing this ship, but the designers never imagined using it for wild parties. The damage however, was minimal during the trip to Earth. The ship landed at the Lunar-Base and was then made ready for the big exploration.

Finally, it left base and headed straight for Earth. The African continent was the first stop, then the eastern Mediterranean area -- where underwater exploration would be done, and then the Caspian Sea area. When observing wildlife, it would hover over areas were humans were not located.

The ship's officers carried out the species selection process in the following manner.

They told individual passengers to select a male and female pair of animals by writing it down on a form. Crewmembers would then use this list to retrieve these animals from the wild. Once the animals were brought on board, they were placed in a zoo and a beauty contest was held as to who chose the most attractive.

When deciding what a beautiful animal is, Regintian standards are different from human ones. Humans would pick a splendidly colored bird or a magnificent looking tiger or zebra. We in contrast, would choose something similar to an orangutan, jellyfish, or crab. The winner would have the privilege of piloting the ship on Earth for a full hour to anywhere he desired after the final exploration of the Mediterranean area.

Finally, the ship arrived in Africa and the sampling began almost immediately. It didn't take long before half the ship was filled with animals -- elephants, giraffes, lions, tigers, buffalos, birds of all types, and of course numerous aquatic species.

The beauty contest was next. The manager running the contest invited everyone to stroll around a zoo-like arena housing all the selections. You could spend hours there; it was that fascinating.

The method of choosing a candidate as the most beautiful species was to allow members of the audience to tick mark their choice on a written form and place it in a box: no fancy computers or counting machines. The next day, in a big ceremony, the contest officials brought the box onto a stage facing a watchful audience as the contest announcer counted the ballots. Who would win the contest . . . crab? Jellyfish? Land animal?

Half an hour later, a medium size cage covered with a blanket was rolled out to center stage, presumably containing the winning animal. Everyone held their breath as they waited for the contest announcer.

"Regintians, the winner is this very lovely animal that is actually related to the human beings on this planet. The creature is . . . the Baboon."

As he said that, the announcer lifted the blanket and there it stood . . . or sat . . . or . . .

No one knew exactly what it was doing but did notice its head pointed to the back of the stage while its behind pointed towards the audience. I don't want to describe what it was doing but let's just say that if a human was in the audience with us at that moment, he definitely would not be indifferent. He would either laugh his head off or look scornfully at the baboon. It wasn't a big deal though, and most people in the audience thought the baboon lovely.

Being a rather small cage, one of the stagehands told the announcer, "Maybe the cage should get cleaned since there's going to be a lot of people wanting to look at this baboon for a long time."

The announcer pointed to him and said, "Ok my friend, why don't you get to work and clean it up."

The stagehand had never done this sort of thing before and indeed no one in that ship on that day had ever been in a cage with any kind of animal before. Despite the fact that the people in the audience were supposed to be Earth studies graduates, people with that kind of experience usually worked in the main exploratory staff on the Earth Station bases around the planet. The stage worker approached the cage with a standard Earth translator that would normally translate Regintian messages into the many human dialects found in that part of Africa where these baboons lived.

The announcer said, "I think that animal understands the most popular dialect in that area. So try it and see what happens."

The worker proceeded to the front door and through the translator told the baboon, "Good day friend, I am going into your cage to clean up the mess. While I'm doing that, I will give you some food, so please stay in the cage. Then I'll leave and close the door, OK?"

There was total silence from the baboon.

"Think he understood me?" asked the stage worker.

"He probably did, so go ahead," said the announcer.

The stagehand calmly opened the door and placed a pile of food near the baboon, then proceeded to scoop up the mess on the floor. Within seconds, the baboon darted out of the cage and began climbing over various objects that were all over the place. Everyone in the audience loved it.

Another stagehand at the back of the stage was ready to shoot the baboon with a stun gun, but the announcer yelled at him and said, "No, don't do that, I think that animal is harmless, and besides the audience loves it."

At that point, the announcer looked at the winner of the contest and said, "Let me take you to the ship's control area and introduce you to the captain."

They both left the hall as everyone continued to admire the baboon. It was still climbing everywhere and jumping over everything.

When they reached the captain's cabin, the captain briefly demonstrated a few basic commands to the winner of the contest that would not allow anything unusual to happen to the ship in case the winner made errors.

"You can take this ship anywhere you want," said the captain.

"I'm not too sure exactly where I want to go; any ideas?" said the winner.

The captain pointed to an Earth map and said, "Just look for some nice looking land masses, like here or here."

He pointed to the boot of Italy and said, "Why not go to that nice boot? It should be fun."

While this was happening, the folks in the zoo-arena were enjoying the wandering baboon. The stagehand mentioned to a co-worker, "Think our friend there might like his female companion; she's over there in that other cage."

As he pointed out the cage, the co-worker mentioned, "I'll open the door and see what happens." The baboon left the cage and immediately headed for her friend.

Someone yelled, "There are other creatures that look like these except they are a lot bigger and appear to be more human like." He was referring to what you would call a chimpanzee.

"Why don't we open those cages and see what happens." So they opened the doors to those two cages, and the chimpanzees slipped out. Within two minutes, they had disappeared.

The announcer finally returned and was appalled by what had been going on. As a party mentality gained impetus, one of the partiers fell in love with the animal he had picked and decided to let him loose. What was this colorful animal people loved?

It was a tiger. What people didn't realize is that the tiger had his eye on one of the chimpanzees, and it wasn't too long before he hunted it down and killed it.

After that happened, the attitude was: how interesting! We are witnessing an Earth-like phenomenon right in our own spaceship, otherwise nothing to worry about. As cages were opened, animals scampered all over the place, and the party was on. People were encouraging the animals to go after and kill other animals. No one tried to stop this except for the announcer, but he was ignored despite his pleas to end the carnage.

While this melee was happening, a lion found its way to the control center since no one considered it dangerous. Everyone admired it as it meandered the corridors of the space ship. People in the control cabin were barely aware of what was going on. The co-pilot, who was aiding the contest winner since the pilot was in the washroom, walked out of the cabin for what was supposedly a few seconds. While that novice pilot continued to control the ship, the co-pilot came across the lion's path. He had no idea about the potential danger and wasn't too sure what to do. He assumed since this lion was let loose along with that tiger, it was probably OK to continue to walk towards it. The lion took his ignorance as an opportunity, and attacked; within seconds, he was killed.

The android pilot had no idea he was dead and since the co-pilot thought he would be back within seconds after he left the cabin, didn't bother setting up a contingency plan for the android. The contest winner told the android to go directly to Italy. The android thought the novice pilot would handle everything correctly and the novice pilot thought the android had everything under control.

Next thing you know the ship entered the Earth's atmosphere at a very high velocity. Normally Regintian spaceships are very durable but that assumes the android controller has complete control over it. At one point, the android controller knew something was not right and decided to bring the ship down. It was a little too late as cracks began to appear in the hull structure and suddenly the landing became an emergency. The android controller concluded he had to ditch the ship since the damage affected the way it flew.

The landing area he chose wasn't exactly the safest, and it ended up being stuck in a crevasse within a small lake in the mountain ranges somewhere in Turkey. Water poured through the cracks while some animals and Regintians escaped and others drowned. The ship quickly began to sink. Eventually, a small group of Regintians managed to land on shore without any long distance communications, except for their usual RF capability.

Some Regintians were stuck out in the middle of the lake hanging onto floating debris. None of the Regintians had cloned human bodies except for one person. He had the foresight to transfer into one as the commotion was spreading.

He was also among the group that reached the shore of the lake, but the human body he was in wasn't in great shape. It had no hair, was extremely skinny, and he had forgotten to bring clothing for it. But it was better than nothing, and he did manage to put some sort of clothing on from all the garbage that was strewn around.

The captain of the cruiser sent out a distress signal and then got together with this person to develop a strategy to save the people out in the middle of the lake while he waited for a rescue vessel. The idea they came up with was to find a boat in a local village, and then go out and get them. Regintians are not great swimmers, and they can drown if the waters are turbulent enough. The captain decided to search for human communities or villagers nearby that could help them. The cloned human would be the one to approach these people. It was a precarious situation considering how the human looked. The cloned human took off with a couple of aids who would stay in the background if they met humans, hiding if they had to.

A pathway through the forest, which later winded its way back along the shoreline, indicated a possible route to a human settlement. They went along it until a small village appeared near a river leading to the lake. The cloned human proceeded slowly and as he approached a dock extending out from the village, noticed a variety of boats from completely broken ones to units that looked like they could barely float.

He noticed a sign on a pole partially hidden by trees. His translator told him it indicated 'used fishing boats'. Aw ha he thought; just what we want. From what he knew of humans, it shouldn't be too hard to bargain with these people if he had anything to trade with.

"Do we have anything to give these people in exchange for their boats?" he said.

"The only thing I can think of is that in some parts of the world they love a certain beverage that happened to be on board the ship. Some of it might have washed up on shore, and we can offer it in exchange for a boat."

They went back to the shore area, searched for these bottles, found one, and proceeded back to the area were the boats were. As he approached a little cabin situated in the middle of this boat area, he could read the complete sign.

It said: 'Noah's used fishing boats'. The cloned human approached the cabin cautiously, and someone emerged. When that person saw the cloned human, he wasn't too sure what to make of it. The cloned human's vocal cords didn't work too well, but he managed to say a weak hello in the local language. Then he pointed to a boat and hoped the person would realize he was interested in a business deal. The person nodded and introduced himself as Shem.

"Hang on, while I get the owner," he said as he went inside the cabin.

"Hey dad, there's some real weird looking dude outside, and I think he wants to buy a boat. But he doesn't seem to speak our language. Maybe you better handle this one."

"What does he look like," responded dad.

"He has no hair whatsoever and looks like he hasn't eaten in days."

Noah grabbed his trousers and as he was putting them on said, "OK I'll handle it."

The cloned human saw an elderly man walk out with Shem and come right up to him.

The elderly man gave a short wave, which probably the way they greeted people in that area and said, "Hi, I'm Noah. Is there anything I can do for you?"

The cloned human pointed to a boat indicating he was interested in it.

Noah said, "You want to buy it?"

The cloned human nodded affirmatively.

Noah looked at his son, "Shem did you see this guy with anyone?"

"Not so far dad."

Noah approached the cloned human, raised his hand, rubbed his thumb and forefinger together, and said, "What kind of an offer can you make?"

The cloned human more or less understood what he wanted and held up both hands, waved them from side to side a bit and then pointed to a wooded area indicating to them that he had to consult with someone there. The cloned human walked over to that area and was back in a few seconds. He brought something with him. From Noah's point of view, it looked like a bottle of liquid. The cloned human made a motion that Noah should drink it. Noah was a bit suspicious.

"I think he wants you to drink it dad."

"Let me take a whiff of this."

Noah pulled the plug from the top of the bottle and smelled it.

"Smells OK. Here you smell this and tell me what you think."

"It smells kinda sweet."

Noah grabbed the bottle back, smelled it again and poured a few drops of it on the back of his hand.

After a bit of licking he proclaimed, "Wow, what a taste. Let me have a little drink." He took a slug of it and said, "Hmmm, this is good. What boat does he want?"

"That one," said Shem as he pointed to one of the boats.

Noah whispered, "Only too happy to get rid of that piece of junk."

Noah now realized that the cloned human couldn't talk, so he held up the bottle with one hand and with the other hand indicated the number five with his fingers. The human smiled and bowed his head indicating he was accepting the deal. There was only one problem; he wouldn't have any of this wine ready until tomorrow since they had only one bottle of it with them and needed to search for more. After a lot of sign language indicating to

Noah that he would be back in a few hours or maybe the next day, the cloned human left.

The next day, the cloned human showed up with all five bottles, and Noah had a big smile on his face.

"Shem, take this guy over to the boat, and let him have it."

"OK, dad. This way my friend; let me show you the boat."

They walked over to it and boarded it. But it was obvious this stranger had no idea what needed to be done to use it. After a lot of hand waving and off the cuff sign language, Shem left the boat and went back to his dad.

"That guy doesn't know a thing about using boats. You might end up losing a customer."

"Or creating one," said Noah, "What we can do is offer him our services . . . at a price."

By this time, one of the five bottles was already empty.

"So how much should we ask for?"

"Let's try another five of these bottles and that will pay for a half day service later this afternoon."

Noah immediately took another slug and burped. Shem sighed, shrugged his shoulders and left the cabin. He walked over to the human and held up his five fingers indicating five more bottles were required to help out with the boat. By this time, the cloned human had already been communicating with his cohorts and told them to get five more bottles ready. Later that afternoon, the cloned human returned with the bottles and was ready for his first lesson, but it didn't happen as both Noah and Shem where intoxicated and asleep and those five first bottles were already empty.

The cloned human saw an opportunity to get all those Regintians on board without any real humans noticing it. He left the extra five bottles he had brought with him near Noah's cabin and then sneaked all ten Regintians on board. All they had to do now was go over to the middle of the lake somewhere and rescue his comrades. There was only one little problem; the boat they boarded was twice as big as the one Noah sold him. Minor detail; they took and launched the larger boat. Since none of them were sailors, they knew nothing about putting up sails. Their only option was to row. That would be good enough since they would only need to do it for about 15 minutes . . . or 30 minutes . . . well maybe 60.

Just as they began to make progress, both Noah and Shem woke up and Shem noticed something, "Hey dad, that boat we sold them is still there." Noah peeked outside and was just about to ask himself why it was still there when he noticed the bigger one missing. He staggered up quickly, rushed outside, and there it was out in the lake, about a kilometer away.

He screamed at the top of his lungs, cursing and swearing and calling them thieves. "Go get your brother while I get this other boat ready. We're going after them."

Shem immediately ran to get his brother Ham and within a few minutes had rushed onto his dad's boat. Noah had one advantage over his customer; he knew what he was doing when it came to sailing. As neighbors began to notice the commotion, they followed Noah with their own boats to back him up.

In the meantime, the so-called refugees were rowing away with all haste, and the Regintian cruiser captain was getting worried when he saw four boats sailing towards him at a much faster clip. He signaled the Regintians floating on the debris that he was almost there, so hang on; they were on their way. It was a matter of minutes.

Suddenly something appeared in the sky . . .

"Dad, what is that light?"

"I have no idea; I've never seen anything like that before," said Noah.

"Hey look, I see something coming out of that light, and it's going down and hovering over our stolen boat," said Ham.

"What the hell are they picking out of the water . . . they look like strange creatures," said Shem, "what's going on here dad?"

Noah was too stunned to say anything. Then miraculously, the stolen boat began to fly towards that radiant object just overhead.

"My God," Noah fell to his knees and began to pray. The people in the other boats fell to their knees as well.

"Oh Lord. Is this the end . . . the final end?" screamed Noah. Noah was now so close to them he could quite clearly see all kinds of strange people on board, devils? Angels? Who knew?

Something else was happening. His boat began shifting around wildly and then started going around in circles. Noah and his sons were terrified . . . screaming . . . panicking.

Up in the rescue spaceship the rescue captain was viewing the whole shebacle. He radioed down to the cruiser captain, "What's going on down there?"

The cruiser captain said, "The boat that is chasing after us is on the edge of the tractor beam that is pulling the rest of us up, so it's losing stability."

"Is it possible that those humans could be in danger?"

Both the rescue captain and the cruiser captain had so little knowledge of human skills and behavior that they weren't too sure if the humans were in any danger at all. The captain on board the rescue ship considered increasing the power to the tractor beam to push the stolen boat out of the way so it would have a reduced effect on Noah's boat, or turn the whole thing off and hope Noah would be scared enough to stop chasing his stolen boat. He decided to go with the riskier move of increasing the tractor beam force while pulling the stolen boat out of the way faster.

It didn't work. Noah's boat briefly angled up into the air with just the bow touching the water and when the rescue captain reduced the tractor beam force, it splashed back into the water resulting in both Noah and his two sons drowning.

It was a sad event. The rescue spaceship didn't bother aiding Noah's boat. It just went off into outer space once it had done its work saving the Regintians.

For the record, our historians attempted to keep track of everything including what religion Noah and his sons belonged to. Unfortunately, even though these partygoers were history students, they didn't pay all that much attention to what was happening, so our information is still unreliable to this very day as there are several religions and cultural traditions claiming Noah's heritage. Was the Spirit Congregation helpful in revealing this information?

Their official answer was to state that Noah and his kin prayed and worshipped their kind, which of course includes God, but did not state which religion or Earth God or gods it could have been. Historic details that are important to later human historians and us are definitely not important to them.

PARTING OF THE RED SEA

Continuing with more Earth events, sometime around 1500 B.C. an unusual incident happened. An inexperienced explorer, piloting a spaceship by himself at nighttime, caused a major accident that year after colliding with another spaceship just above the ground. They crashed into a deep marsh causing the exploration management to send a team of rescuers to retrieve the ship.

The next step was to setup a special Monitoring Station in that marsh to prevent leakage from it into the Red Sea. An experience veteran, named Missingarg, led this team. When Missingarg arrived at the scene, he and his team saw a badly damaged eco-system. He reported the matter to the Lunar-Base and ordered down large rescue vessels to remove the damaged ship, prevent the water from leaking, and restore the marsh to a reasonable condition. Just before they brought the siphoning equipment out, someone noticed a large assemblage of people in the far distance walking towards the damaged environment.

At first, they thought their disastrous accident had attracted curiosity seekers from the surrounding area. Missingarg responded by sending a probe out to determine the nature of this human accumulation. The report that came back had determined that thousands of people called Hebrews, who normally worked on the Egyptian Empire's large buildings (like pyramids etc), were starting to accumulate near the edge of that marsh leakage. That certainly put a lid on our plan to restore the marsh and retrieve the spaceship. Why would these people suddenly show up here?

There was too many of them to justify the theory that they were mere curiosity seekers. Infiltrating the group with one of our clones became a prime objective to figure out what was going on. After mingling with these Hebrews, we found out they were here not because of us, but because of a bad political and economic situation created by the Egyptian authorities. Their goal was to leave Egypt and proceed east towards an area that is commonly referred to as Israel or Canaan, but that marsh leakage was blocking them.

Just as our agent began making headway to gain the confidence of the Hebrew leadership, a huge army of Egyptian soldiers arrived ready to make war and slaughter them. Our agent concluded that if our work in this marsh wasn't done quickly, we were going to be right in the middle of this battle. Missingarg convened an emergency meeting in the lead spaceship, located in the marsh area, to determine what the next step should be. He was well aware of the human penchant for violence, and this impending disaster might end up being a demonstration of that. Our policy of non-interference had to be maintained without having these people slaughtered, especially in the area we were working.

A solution might be to have that agent of ours become a confidant of their leader, but it wasn't as easy as we thought since there appeared to be several leaders representing the Hebrews. Each one had their own way of doing things with different interpretations as to why they were there and how the Egyptians were treating them. We were getting nowhere and were running out of time trying to solve this problem.

Missingarg and his staff were now so desperate that he thought a little bit of manipulation wouldn't violate our 'non-interference' policy with humans since the marsh leakage we caused might be creating an unwanted problem to begin with. Here is the solution he came up with.

Once we confirmed that these people all had the same religion, the goal would be to inject a leader to unite them, affirm that he was sent by God to lead them, and then quickly remove them from the marsh area.

The rescue mission explained all this to the Spirit Congregation, and they gave their approval. They really didn't care what happened. If everyone were slaughtered, they'd welcome them all into the afterlife and then sort them out later. If they weren't slaughtered, the Hebrews would still pray to God and satisfy the Spirit Congregation's 'appetite for worship'. Both Egyptians and Hebrews worshiped them and as far as they were concerned, they didn't prefer either culture. When Hebrews pray to God, it is He that is on the receiving end of the prayers. If the Egyptians worshiped the sun god, it is still God on the receiving end, if some saint or prophet, then a major angel took control.

For the next step, I wish the rescue team had done a better job. Missingarg decided to use a different agent to infiltrate the Hebrews; his name was Ursad -- an explorer who had an unreliable reputation. One of the problems we have in determining how to send our explorers to Earth is the amount of influence you have with the Brotherhood, not how competent you are as an explorer. For the most part, I would say that the majority of our explorers on Earth and on the Lunar-Base are quite capable, but Ursad was different. He certainly wasn't incompetent, fairly intelligent in fact, but was egocentric and rarely followed orders.

Missingarg was well aware of the 'clout' Ursad had with the Brotherhood. Ursad's instructions were to enter the disaster area in his regular human cloned body, befriend the Hebrew people, guide them out of the marsh, and then lead them to wherever they desired. Missingarg told him specifically not to get too 'magical'. Use only as little high technology as possible to convince the people that he was a holy person. Maybe predict the weather or some innocuous thing like that as opposed to using anti-gravity devices that fly around or using 3D viewers and other high technology. Think he'd take this advice? No.

Ursad was an excitable person and when he arrived in that area, he used every little gimmick he could imagine to convince them he was a great prophet. It wasn't difficult predicting how easily they fell for it. Ursad always carried with him a staff that appeared to be made out of wood. It had 3D projected technology built into it, so he could flash 3D images all over the place giving it a miracle-like experience. Rather than go around to the different tribal leaders and reason with them, he decided to stand on a donkey cart and use it as a pedestal to summon the Hebrew people. Then he used his staff's built in loudspeaker system and introduced himself as Moses.

Ursad's ego amazed us. But there wasn't time to rein his behavior in since stopping the leakage was the priority. Once that got underway -- using anti-gravity, siphoning, and fast evaporation methods -- it wasn't too long before we stopped the leakage and removed the spaceship.

Before the Egyptian soldiers could do anything, Ursad (now Moses) quickly led the Hebrew people across the now drained leakage area and after they had passed, we immediately let it leak again to prevent those soldiers from catching and slaughtering them.

Monitoring stations on Earth, as well as on the moon, were closely observing these events. It was quite a relief when everyone crossed the marsh without any violence on either side. The next step was to analyze the impact our interference might have on human development. During a long meeting at the Lunar-Base, we analyzed this information and concluded it wouldn't have any -- really!

If our spaceship hadn't crashed, the Hebrews would have had quick access to where they were heading and possibly avoided the confrontation. Then again, crashing and not interfering would definitely have caused a slaughter. Our designated intervention of supporting the Hebrew people offset our accidental interference. This pretext left our conscience clear.

The next potential problem was Ursad. Some of us were worried about him, but our expedition leader assured us that he would be back at headquarters within a few days.

That . . . just didn't happen!

Next thing you know, he's leading the Hebrews across the desert, inspiring, cajoling, and pushing them to go beyond any previous peaceful mandate they may have had when leaving Egypt. The Hebrew's new mandate was to conquer the land by any means possible. If this meant mass slaughter for example, so be it.

At one time when Moses made his way up a small mountain to visit a shuttle-craft we were using as a mobile station, he came into contact with a 'standard' angel sent by the Congregation to ensure he was in accord with their way of 'spirit direction'. Moses told the angel he had no objection with what they wanted, although I'm not too sure why the angel believed him since he was not able to read Moses' mind -- not having a 'guardian angel'. The angel seemed satisfied that Moses was more or less in accordance with their way of doing things.

Once that little encounter was out of the way, Moses proceeded into the shuttle-craft with the enthusiasm of a geek visiting a hi-tech store in the 21st century. One of the gimmicks he was in search of was a couple of what 21st century humans would call a tablet computer (at least twice as long as the Apple iPad). When he entered the shuttle, he grabbed a couple of large ones without Missingarg's approval. His goal was to place images or videos on these tablets as a way of maintaining his power over the Hebrews.

During the many days he was on the mountain, a few of the now displaced leaders that Moses had demoted by his convincing presence as a holy person, persuaded some of the Hebrew people to worship another figure or deity. When Moses returned, he was outraged and given his egocentricity, used the high-tech ability of the Tablets to realign the Hebrews back towards him. How did he do this?

In combination with his usual 'magical' staff and the images he was now flashing across his tablets, he persuaded a small group of his followers to go forth and slaughter many fellow Hebrews (idolaters he called them). Since we were following this situation in real-time, we swarmed him with nanobots effectively paralyzing him, consequently ending the slaughter.

To be quite honest with you, Missingarg, and especially the exploration management staff on the lunar base, were devastated. A case could be made that we Regintians, along with Missingarg, were directly involved with the murder of these people by allowing this person to have this power. Our reaction was swift and predictable. We removed both Ursad and Missingarg from Earth and managed to persuade the Hebrews to get a new leader from among their own people -- with guidance from the Spirit Congregation. They promised us, after all this, they would leave this new leader alone.

A seemingly bizarre event was about to unfold in the next few days. To our utmost surprise, Ursad reappeared amongst the Hebrews and continued to lead them for the longest time. This was the Spirit Congregation at their most devious. After their agreement with us to leave the Hebrew people alone, except for minor guidance, they somehow brought him back to Earth to continue to lead them. The expedition management's attitude was to wipe their hands and ignore the whole situation. They didn't want to get into a battle with the Spirit Congregation.

Ursad's leadership more or less continued for many years along the same lines -- from passionate tenderness to gargantuan atrocities. The Congregation backed any form of spirit adoration, not just individual religions like Hebrew or pharaoh worship. They still thought that Ursad would be a good agent for focusing the Israeli people's adoration on them.

There came a time however when even the Spirit Congregation became a little worried. Normally, they loved anyone who inspired humans to worship them but were worried that Moses might end up posing himself as a god. Ursad, begin Regintian, could live for an extremely long time. As the Hebrew leader for 120 Earth years, the so-called 'standard angel' had a meeting with him and pointed out that he might be encouraging god-like worship towards him rather than human admiration.

That was the excuse the Spirit Congregation used to finally remove him from his exalted position. The expedition management finally removed him from Earth and sent him to Reginta. The Spirit Congregation had been trying to persuade us to let him die so they could deal with him. This little debate of what to do with him became rather mute when Ursad escaped with the help of collaborators.

He was found about a hundred years later, guess where? . . . More on that later.

About a thousand years later, someone from one of our Monitoring Stations (in the usual cloned body) was poking around an ancient library somewhere in the Middle East and stumbled onto religious documentation citing a body of water called the Reed Sea. After a thorough reading of it, it dawned on him that these records were describing the parting of the Red Sea by one of your deities during the Moses time period; I believe it was the Jewish God.

Most human history books later cited that marsh were our spaceship crash landed as the Red Sea. The documentation that our person saw stated it was the Sea of Reeds. Even this wasn't quite accurate since it was a marsh after all. The climate in those days was slightly different than it was in the 20th century.

It was obvious he was reading about the event of the Hebrews escaping from the army of Egyptian soldiers. There were a few exaggerations in this particular documentation. The Egyptian soldiers did not drown nor did any of them die throughout this ordeal. When they saw the waters receding near the marsh, these soldiers were too confused to do anything so just stood there and gazed. The document went on and on praising a person called Moses. However, it did confirm the slaughter event after he had descended Mount Sinai. Did our actions in those days make us part of an Earth religion? After that incident, a certain amount of soul searching took place where we had to be more careful in the future whenever we interfaced with humans.

Overall, the Spirit Congregation thought the whole episode wonderful since it would encourage humans to continue to worship and pray to them. They must love this particular document.

MESOPOTAMIA

Continuing with our Moses event, let me carry on with the story of his escape from the spaceship carrying him back to Reginta. I will quickly summarize it as unfortunately, we don't have a great deal of information about this incident.

When Ursad returned to Earth, he befriended someone in the Marduk court of Mesopotamia, bragging that he was a god after demonstrating to him that tablet computer.

Even though he was warned many times in the past not to do this, he dazzled them with its ability to project 3D displays. He also demonstrated his ability to produce stone reliefs by using a programmable laser designed to etch almost any type of material. Ursad created the above picture of a stone relief, which is attributed to the Mesopotamians. He expected they would admire and venerate him; instead, they tried to kill him.

Out of desperation, he got rid of his cloned body hoping his alien form would inspire them to revere him. At first, it seemed to work but later on, they still killed him. Once we found the fatality scene, we quickly retrieved his body to prevent any biological evidence from being left behind.

Many centuries later, the Spirit Congregation revealed it had actually persuaded the Mesopotamians to kill him through the current deity they worshiped. The Congregation didn't wish for a rival deity in the form of Ursad, by then a lowly Regintian in their minds.

Let's just say it was an incident which didn't upset us too much since it's a problem we don't have to worry about anymore. Ursad is now completely in the hands of the Spirit Congregation and we have no idea of his status.

THE GREAT WALL OF CHINA

I would like to introduce you to Eubas, but before I do that let's check with the spirit to see if he's finished praying. Eubas, can you open that door to find out?

Eubas is my young nephew, and I promised I'd allow him some time here as a present for his 'Awareday' -- a celebration like your birthday. It won't take too long as this event is just a summary.

That's it; just open it up and take a peek.

I BELIEVE IN THY HOLINESS

AND THY GREATNESS

WITH ALL THY...

. . . and of course close it since he's still at it. We'll just stay in the present room.

Eubas fancies speaking directly to you in your language without support from any translation equipment. He is currently in a Regintian avatar and will try to produce sounds from the vibration capability in his eyelids. He's been practicing this for months and does get better every time he comes here.

Go ahead Eubas; try your audible language skills again to explain the Great Wall of China to this human.

Goo. .- Ea..h…g. My n..e is --bas.

Most -- -he time, --r past e.pl-rers di- ma.age -- st-y out o- sight. -- -- an..her part of the w..ld, yet ano--- u.fort…te i--ident ha--ened. One of our -----t -xp--rers had the idea of crea.ing a perm--nt st.u-ture -n --ur pla.et and d…uise i. as a hu--n d---ling so it w--ld -lend ri.ht in .. the sur-ou-din--s.

OK Eubas. Just hang on a sec here. Once again, I don't think your verbalization skills are up to this human's standards so if you could please switch over into the standard translation procedures, I think we would both appreciate it.

Good day Earthling, my name is Eubas.

Most of the time, our past explorers did manage to stay out of sight but in another part of the world, yet another unfortunate incident happened. One of our ancient explorers had the idea of creating a permanent structure on your planet and disguising it as a human dwelling so it could blend right in with the surroundings.

Using spaceships for Monitoring Stations was a bit tiresome considering they weren't adaptable to all possible conditions found on Earth. Hopefully, this 'Earthly' facility wouldn't attract too much attention, and humans would leave us alone. Furthermore, our explorers noticed how territorial humans had become and thought that if they appeared 'territorial' enough with this structure, humans would keep their distance.

Chinese civilization at this time in history was fairly developed, and we thought it was an ideal place for a new Base Station. After it was finished, it wasn't too long before humans began building their own settlements nearby.

This was a nuisance to us, so our explorers decided to scare the humans away by manipulating the weather and causing storms. It worked, at least for a couple of months. Next thing you know, the humans attacked them. They certainly had no desire to fight the humans since it would be no contest, and Regintians are not the type of beings who fancied killing them.

The explorers devised yet another solution and built a wall around their little headquarters rather than move, which would have been an annoyance. It worked, and it did prevent further attacks from those people. The wall was so effective, it inspired someone

on their side to also build a defensive wall against invading armies from the north. Over the next few years, the wall continued to grow and grow for vast distances.

This is now called the Great Wall of China and is one of the great ancient structures on Earth. It is so admired by humans of all cultures that we have a certain element of pride in our influence (or interference).

Thanks for listening Earthling; I will now turn you back to Uncle Appleton.

Thank you Eubas; keep practicing.

And there you have it, a quick explanation of one of the great archeological events in human history, all done to solve the annoyance of moving a Monitoring Station around.

I was supposed to turn you over to Erborite for the next two stories but he hasn't shown up yet. This might be a time for you to go to the washroom or get yourself a drink from the fridge.

We'll see you next paragraph.

LOCKNESS MONSTER

Hello Earthling; my name is Erborite.

While you were on a break to the washroom or the fridge, or simply flipping the page, Appleton went outside the room and hasn't returned yet. This happens with almost every human that makes an appearance here and is becoming a ritual. So I'll just go ahead and start without him.

I am going to present you with a bizarre piece of history that has provoked the human imagination for generations, and it all happened in a single location in Scotland. Let me direct you to the large wall display at the back of the room. On this screen, I'll demonstrate why the legend of the so-called Lockness monster survived for so long.

This incident began when Permontague, one of our novice and arrogant explorers, longed to explore the deep oceans of Earth for intelligent life. The current leader at the time of the existing Earth expedition -- a person named Monston Waterbee -- told him there was no way the waters of Earth had intelligent species. Permontague was as stubborn and obstinate as they come. He was also well connected with a lot of influence back on our home planet and as usual, these people got their way.

Let me demonstrate. While he was preparing this 'adventure' of his, a special combination underwater and outer space vessel suddenly appeared in orbit around the moon in the year 565 A.D. It looked oddly similar to the so-called Noah's ark cruiser from a few hundred years ago, but a bit smaller. This was completely unexpected and revealed the connections he had with wealthy family members on Reginta.

When Monston saw this, he more or less kept his distance from Permontague. *Let him do what he wants* was the thinking. Within a week, Permontague took control of it, went underwater, and wasn't heard from for a long time. Here are a few of the comments made by Monston in the official logs of the expedition.

"Over a year goes by and we don't hear a thing from this guy. I also want to make a little confession here. We didn't even consider sending out a rescue mission; I mean nobody cared about him because they couldn't stand him.

"Then out of nowhere, a radio message was received from his vessel just north of Scotland. What was his excuse for this disappearance? He claimed to have been exploring the north Atlantic for about a year and merely stated that he wasn't aware of any rules stipulating he had to call in every once in a while. Nobody, but nobody, believed what he was saying. He lied just so he wouldn't lose face for getting lost."

Later on, Monston set in motion a small inquiry which determined that Permontague had gone astray and wasn't able to fly the ship out of the water because of a power breakdown. Permontague still refused to admit failure.

The final report concluded:

"The vessel breakdown was caused by a power failure. Permontague refused all rescue assistance and attempted to unsuccessfully fix the problem himself. The vessel was still functional underwater, and he was able to maneuver it to a place now called Beauly Firth in Scotland."

Getting back to this chronicle, once he arrived at that place, Permontague thought everything was under control, and tried to repair the vessel himself. The vessel continued to drift underwater while he persisted in making it flight-worthy. Unfortunately, severe storms were a constant companion and since the vessel wasn't capable of diving any deeper, the huge waves in the firth impeded the repair effort.

Permontague's scans of the local area resulted in the discovery of an inland body of water that had less surface movement than the Beauly Firth. His next problem was getting the vessel over there without humans noticing it and without our help. Floating up the river Ness, appeared to be relatively easy. When that course of action began, he noticed humans on the riverbank and immediately submerged to avoid observation.

Unfortunately, just before he did that, he hit something on the surface, which turned out to be a fishing boat. The sensors on the submerged vessel indicated that humans on board the boat underwent major harm including some injured person falling overboard.

They now had an emergency on their hands. One of Permontague's crewmembers -- who wasn't in a cloned body -- considered going outside to rescue the injured person, while wearing only a Regintian scuba-diving outfit. This was a risky move; if they saw him, he would appear to be a strange beast since people living in the year 565 A.D. were more apt to be superstitious.

Without considering the consequences, the crewmember went outside anyway, but it was too late; the human had already drowned. He attempted to drag the body to the shoreline without being noticed. It almost happened except for the fact that the dead person's companions were searching for him, and one was already swimming in the water to get his body.

He was suddenly faced with a dilemma. If he let the body go, it was at the point where it would sink. If he held on to it, that rescuer might notice him, which could cause the rescuer to panic. So the crewmember held on to the body and stayed underwater waiting for the rescuer to grab it.

Within a minute, the rescuer reached them and right behind him was the boat. Unfortunately, since the crewmember was underwater, he didn't see the boat and when the swimmer grabbed the body, our guy began to move away pretty sure he hadn't been noticed.

Next thing you know, someone hit him with an oar. He didn't know if it was intentional or if the human controlling that oar was trying to steady the boat and accidentally hit him. In any case, our person lost his sense of direction and surfaced. When that happened, the people in the boat panicked and some even jumped overboard. He appeared to be a horrible monster to them.

The crewmember lowered himself back into the water and returned to our vessel. That whole adventure hadn't been worth it. The crewmember had been 'slapped around' a bit, Permontague had his ego bruised, and then the really bad news surfaced.

After working on the vessel, they discovered it was irreparable and notified Headquarters. They reluctantly admitted they had a defective ship on their hands. In the next 24 hours or so, a rescue vessel arrived in the middle of the night with the intention of salvaging the ship and taking its crew back to headquarters. This was supposed to be a strait forward operation, but something went wrong again. The rescuers did manage to descend and lock on to the damaged ship but when they tried to lift it, it wouldn't give. It was stuck in a crevasse and for them to remove it, they would have had to shift some of the underlying strata.

By the time they had surfaced and figured out what to do, the sun had risen over the horizon, and a large flotilla of fishing boats unexpectedly appeared from the local villages. A person jumped off one of them and began swimming towards both the rescue ship and Permontague's vessel.

In the meantime, while we were observing this on one of our display screens, a leader or religious figure with a symbolic staff pointed towards the water and pronounced something. Let's just say it was not an opportune time to continue this rescue mission.

The following night, with fishing boats not present, they removed both ships without any interference. On return to our orbiting headquarters, we discovered that the Spirit Congregation had been in contact with that leader and had motivated him to go forth and inspire his people. The whole purpose of this exercise was to encourage the locals to pray to members of the Spirit Congregation allowing them to obtain a few more religious brownie points.

There was nothing we could have done about this escapade since the Treaty of Spiritual Truth didn't cover every situation and contingency between humans and us.

Eventually, that leader was rewarded for his efforts by acquiring the title of saint -- Saint Columba that is.

Saint Adomnán of Iona (627–704 A.D.) documents this in his 'Life of St. Columba'. He referred to that crewmember as a water beast. The rest of this work is not very accurate, but this is where the Loch Ness monster legend begins.

It continues to this very day.

Appleton?

THE BATTLE WITH THE SPIRIT CONGREGATION

Thank you Erborite.

Erborite is going to explain to you another incident in a few seconds. I wish to direct you to another part in the museum where he will describe to you an event that happened in 1561. I don't know if you're familiar with this, but I'm revealing it to you for the record.

Go ahead Erborite.

Thank you Appleton and hello again human.

This so-called battle over Nuremberg depicted in this picture around 1561 was a complete misunderstanding on our part.

At the time, we had an officer on board one of our vessels who had an incredible dislike for the Spirit Congregation. He had no intention of ever going to heaven and their presence on Earth upset him. As far as he was concerned, the Congregation yearned to constantly exploit the religious potential of human beings. Other than that officer, our relations with them are usually good except for the odd little irritating scenario, which would happen occasionally.

In 1561, a series of seismic studies around Europe was underway and large cylinders needed to be planted in deep underground caves near Nuremberg. The manager controlling this operation erred when he

allowed this anti-Congregation officer to install these cylinders. A second mistake followed; instead of that officer delivering these cylinders at night when the probably of discovery would be low, he delivered them in the middle of the day.

When the local people saw a couple of spaceships delivering these cylinders to their area, panic set in as the leaders alerted their armies. There was one little problem; were these local people gawking the forces of good, or the forces of evil? Some of the more religious people went down on their knees and began to pray at what they saw, other people thought they were witnessing the devil and ran away from their homes taking all their families with them.

It wasn't too long before the Congregation contacted the top management of our entire expedition (using their usual subconscious inter-dimensional techniques) to seek our viewpoint on the situation, since it was us that had instigated the operation. Our project administrator told them he wanted to end the panic among the people cause by the misuse of our spaceships. Now here was the tricky part. We were intrigued to find out if they could curtail this panic by using a simple little miracle technique, without exploiting the situation for 'worship potential' beyond what was normally acceptable. So we held our breath when we went along with their idea of placating the people effected with a few miracles which would hopefully be interpreted as something good and stabilizing, and get back to normal.

What miracle did they conjure? They allowed certain people's minds (the ones with the guardian angels) into believing they were witnessing a great battle between the forces of good and evil. This was the usual mind control effort and in this unsophisticated (unscientific) era of human development, it was good enough for just a sizable minority of people to be affected by it.

And the rest who didn't see it -- since there wasn't enough guardian angels to go around on short notice -- just went along with the others. In our estimation, the great battle these people thought they witnessed was way over done and in the long run, counterproductive.

The Congregation didn't seem to care one way or another as long as they got their worshipers.

Thank you Erborite.

MAYAN KNOWLEDGE

If you bought this book in the year 2012, you are probably aware of all the so-called end of times prophecies based on discredited Mayan historical records. I will now clear this mess up for you. All the information the Mayans produced based on their so-called calendar was actually bestowed on them, and their predecessors the Olmec, by one of our escaped prisoners!

Just like humans, we are not perfect and every once in a while someone does something illegal. Since our explorers are very far away from Reginta and still far away from administrative stations on the Lunar-Base when they are on Earth, it's tiresome if someone breaks the law. Our authorities have to imprison them either in an orbiting vessel or on a special Lunar-Base location.

Rashtahaha was one explorer who had a lot of trouble following orders, and one day he had to be imprisoned in that location near the Lunar-Base. He had to stay there until one of our spaceships returned to either Reginta or another administrative outpost that had a proper prison.

Well guess what? That moon based prison wasn't exactly well guarded (we average one prisoner every two thousand years) and was relatively easy to break out of. It wasn't until two days later that the so-called 'competent' prison administrators noticed the escape. Since the amount of prisoners we get is so incredibly small, the best way of describing our prison officials when it came to supervising these people, is that they were usually 'out of practice'.

The authorities attempted to track him back to Earth but were unable to do so despite advanced technology used in sensing virtually any organism we desired. This continued for centuries and eventually, he became a footnote in history.

Sometime around the year 1702, our expedition management appointed a new mission leader named Masuratza. After reviewing our entire expeditionary procedure, Masuratza concluded that we were a little short in our knowledge of Central and South American history. Our previous expeditions appeared to have popped in and out of that area after establishing monitoring bases for about twenty years, and then pulling them out for a couple of hundred or so. No great focus on these civilizations obviously. There was more interest in Europe, and the middle and Far East, than in this region.

Masuratza expanded the existing base in Central America and was determined to keep it there on a more permanent basis. He eventually stationed five people there, all with human cloned bodies of course. As usual, they mixed and associated with all the existing cultures, including the new Spanish colonists.

One of the local cultures they wished to focus on were people called the Mayans. Many years ago, their civilization broke down. Even though we knew about these people, our ignorance of this culture became an embarrassment considering our so-called dedication to learning about all human development.

As supervisor of this Station, Masuratza was fascinated with this ancient Mayan culture and thought the best way of familiarizing himself with these people was with some of the more scholarly Spanish colonists that were settling in.

Francisco Ximénez was a Dominican friar from Spain widely known for his knowledge of a certain Mayan culture named Popol Vuh. Popol Vuh is a narrative of creation, ancestry, history, and cosmology of the Post Classic K'iche' kingdom in Guatemala's western highlands.

The Spanish conquered these people in 1524. Masuratza met Francisco Ximénez in 1703 and at first considered him to be an interesting acquaintance. As they became acquainted, Francisco invited Masuratza to his office to examine all of the ancient Mayan documentation he had accumulated over the years. I will now play a recording of Masuratza, created just after Francisco passed away, describing his meeting with him.

I found Francisco to be very friendly and accommodating. We became very close. He was so friendly he even enjoyed my humor. And, if you can enjoy a Regintian's humor then you certainly must be friendly. Not only was Francisco interested in converting the locals to his religion, he was also fascinated with their history and was totally dedicated to documenting it. He had numerous friends amongst the locals in that area and intended to learn as much about their ancient history as possible.

I lied to him (as usual) and told him I was a history professor in Italy that wished to set up a study in a major university there about ancient cultures all across the Americas. He was overjoyed to hear that and enthusiastically revealed to me his storehouse of documentation about the Mayans and their history.

After about an hour, an ancient painting of an indigenous holy figure dressed in a very colorful costume emerged from his collection. When I first saw it, I held back a snigger as it looked like a Regintian wearing a tribal outfit. The more I stared at it, the more it dawned on me that it was a rather strange co-incidence that this ancient painting did indeed resemble a Regintian.

Then Francisco showed me several layers of parchments used as writing material and when I closely scrutinized them, I did a double take. I immediately recognized the symbology as a Regintian alphabet used by one of our cultures back on our home planet of Reginta. My memory drew me to the Rashtahaha person who had escaped our prison a long time ago and was never found . . . until now!

Francisco had been trying to translate this for years but to no avail. It was different from anything he's ever seen in the local cultures. The writing was considered an ancient deity script and untranslatable. I asked Francisco if I could have a quick look at it, and he said fine. Having an excellent memory, I managed to memorize several pages before I finished reading it.

This is what I read.

The old traditions of this place start in a place called Quiché. Here we shall write and begin the old stories of all that was done in the town of the Quiché, by the tribes of the Quiché nation. And here we shall state and decree all that was hidden, the revelation by . . . . .

Some of this I couldn't understand. There were many references to places and people of their ancient past and without having enough scholarship in this area, it was pointless trying to understand it all. I lied again and told him I couldn't understand any of it. The last thing I wanted was for him to find out about the Regintian alphabet.

I set the document aside, and Francisco discussed with me his narrative efforts in detailing the 'Quiche' history and folklore. He pulled a manuscript written in Spanish out of a cabinet and allowed me to read some of the work. I began to flip through the pages and noticed that the beginning was similar to the beginning of that Regintian script.

THIS IS THE BEGINNING of the old traditions of this place called Quiché. Here we shall write and we

110

shall begin the old stories, the beginning and the origin of all that was done in the town of the Quiché, by the tribes of the Quiché nation. And here we shall set forth the revelation, the declaration, and the narration of all that was hidden, the revelation by . . . . .

Similar? Wait a minute . . . it was way too similar. I read it over again and could see that at the end of the third sentence, which I will show you next, the rhythm and cadence were the same even if the words of places and people were different. This was probably because there is no formal translation of names when translating between Regintian and Spanish alphabets. Continuing in Spanish with that last sentence:

. . . and the narration of all that was hidden, the revelation by Tzacol, Bitol, Alom, Qaholom, who are called Hunahpú-Vuch, Hunahpú-Utiú, Zaqui-Nimá-Tziís, Tepeu, Gucumatz, u Qux cho, u Qux Paló, Ali Raxá Lac, Ah Raxá Tzel, as they were called.

The Regintian dialogue had the words 'the revelation' and 'who are called' in exactly the same place amongst those names as the Spanish sentence.

Whoa, I thought. Was Rashtahaha the source and instigator of this religion? I felt like I was on to a major discovery. I still didn't want Francisco to know that I had any knowledge to add to his research. How was I going to read more of that Rashtahaha document without drawing a lot of attention to myself?

An opportunity arose when Francisco stepped out of the room to go to the washroom. While he was out, I quickly scrutinized it somewhere in the middle, and this is extracted from a few key days of Rashtahaha's experience:

Day 1.

I have arrived in a place the local people call Quiché, and I think I will stay here for a while and make it my home. When I escaped from prison, I managed to sneak

111

out a fancy hand held 3D projection device. You just never know, this could come in handy when dealing with the local people here. I also have a weapon but that is mostly for defense against animals and possibly humans if they resort to violence.

Day 2.

Entering a local village this morning has attracted a lot of attention. I was unable to escape prison with my human cloned body, so I decided to dress up in a fancy tribal uniform to hide most of my Regintian physiology. I don't speak their language very well because most of my linguistic skills through my translator were devoted to European languages. But I should be proficient enough in a couple of days to effectively communicate with them.

In the meantime, how can I become an influential person amongst this tribe? It might be easier than I thought since some of them are actually kneeling down as I walk pass them. Off in the distance, I notice a couple of warrior class humans with spears in their hands. No surprise there since I might appear to be a little threatening to them being a disguised Regintian and all.

Just behind them is presumably a leader or maybe even the official head of government, whatever that could be. I am going to be very friendly and make creative use of that 3D projection device I have.

Day 100.

The leader has now made me one of his closest advisers and doesn't make a move without my advice.

Day 125.

I am now so close to the leader that he wants me to sleep with at least three of his wives. I had to laugh at myself when he told me this, there is no way a Regintian person can have sex with a human female, so I have absolutely no desire to have sex with anyone least of all the leader's wives.

Day 126.

The leader is very upset that I didn't have sex with any of them. He feels insulted that I didn't find them attractive even though he does. He takes it as a personal affront to his taste in women. I have to find a solution by this evening or else I'm in big trouble.

So here is the plan; one of my servants will sneak into the sleeping chamber when it is very dark, and he will have sex with one of the wives and hopefully it will be so dark the wife will not know it's not me. Let's see what happens.

Day 127.

This morning the servant, and that leader's wife he slept with, is nowhere to be seen. Oh dear . . . what to do now?

When I entered the bedroom, one of my other servants was waiting for me and told me he saw him leaving the enclosure and building with the wife. Then someone else saw them scrambling into the village arm in arm. This happened at dawn.

First question I ask myself is: was she abducted or did she go willingly.

Second question is: should I go after them? What will the leader think?

Day 128.

Today I will meet with the leader, and I plan to inform him I am so much in love with his wife, could he give her to me. Later in the day, I asked him, and he answered with a big smile on his face and said, "Yes, by all means, please take her she's yours."

Boy was I happy when that plan worked so well.

Then he said, "Bring her over here; I want to see her and wish her eternal happiness."

I said, "Errr. . . yyyyes, I'll go and get her." I left the room and didn't bother coming back for hours. Dealing with humans is always so complicated. They are so unpredictable and each one thinks differently. This leader thinks he owns everyone and everything.

So I came up with another plan. I found someone that resembled her, and told her to be very quiet and deferential to the leader and play along with everything that was said. My thinking here was that this person has slept with so many women that he might not recognize her, and I'd be off the hook.

I brought the girl into his chamber, and he reacted exactly the way I predicted. He didn't recognize her. He gave her a kiss on the cheek and wished her happiness.

Day 250.

It's been 250 days since I arrived here, and I am fed up with this leader. It would be easy to take over his leadership, and I thought *why don't I just go ahead and do it?* Most of his servants and administrators were on board; they all hated him. It would be an easy thing to do: simply aim a laser weapon at him and poof, he dies.

Day 252.

So that's it, the leader is now dead, and I am the new leader. When I first arrived here, I thought about educating these people into a modern scientific society, but now I've changed my mind. I will not do that. Even though I disagree with the Brotherhood's philosophy on a lot of things, I generally agree with them about leaving humans alone.

But the situation is slightly different now; I want to influence these people in my own way without the Regintian expedition finding out about it. So it makes sense that my influence will stay subdued; in other words just high enough to affect them in a positive way but not so high as to attract attention from the odd Regintian explorer that may show up once in a while.

I have only translated a few pages. It's just as well it's untranslatable for humans. Rashtahaha had evolved the document into a personnel diary. Even though the likelihood of humans translating this document is nil, I would not expect their translating skills to stay the same over long periods of time. After

all, we've been observing them for over 45,000 years and can see that human progress and knowledge is increasing steadily century by century.

Could it be in the future that humans would acquire enough skill and knowledge to translate this? I am not sure, but I concluded that this has to be removed from Francisco's possession and claimed for our own archives.

Just before I put the document away, I placed spy nanobots into the pages to keep track of it. When the opportunity arises, either my colleagues or I will attempt to secretly remove this document so no one will be the wiser. We are also going to censor a lot of it once it gets into our possession.

How did Rashtahaha manage to hide all these years since he didn't even have a cloned human body? It was obvious he took refuge in a disguise by designing a suit that was human like and was the basis for the colossal head artwork. He continued to influence the Mayans during their classic period once the Olmec had more or less declined. Eventually Rashtahaha disappeared and that was when the Mayan civilization ended.

Oh and one other little mystery needs to be solved. Is Rashtahaha still alive? My feeling is that he is dead, but there is no scientific proof of this. At the present time, we have an entirely new expedition management, and they are on the watch.

This is Appleton again.

Rashtahaha's diary is now in our hands. It was shortly after Francisco had passed away that Masuratza sneaked into the place where he lived and simply walked away with that diary. We might release the complete document after making proper contact with Earth authorities.

After reading Masuratza's report, the exploration management was shocked. This interference by Rashtahaha was deliberate. When we found out they worshiped him as a god, it made us wonder why the Spirit

Congregation didn't inform us about what happened. After all, they want to make sure that only *they* are worshiped by humans.

Just before I finish this section on Mayan culture, I am sure that you are wondering what all the 2012 disaster talk is about. For those people who believe in these fairy tales I will summarize the truth by quoting the on-line encyclopedia Wikipedia.

"Scholars from various disciplines have dismissed the idea of such cataclysmic events occurring in 2012. Professional Mayanist scholars state that predictions of impending doom are not found in any of the extant classic Maya accounts, and that the idea that the Long Count calendar "ends" in 2012 misrepresents Maya history and culture. Astronomers and other scientists have rejected the proposals as pseudoscience, stating that they conflict with simple astronomical observations and amount to "a distraction from more important science concerns, such as global warming and loss of biological diversity"."

"2012 phenomenon." Wikipedia, The Free Encyclopedia.

Couldn't of put it better myself. This is the end of the stories we wish to inform you about up until the 20th century.

INTRODUCING OUR EXHIBITS

Now I'll take you to a more traditional part of the museum.

Please follow me through this entrance and within a moment, you'll notice many familiar items depending how well you did as a history student. . . . .

...I BELIEVE IN YOU OH LORD MOST HIGH...

Opps, sorry wrong door; it's the entrance on the other side.

It's traditional in the sense that we have taken great care to make it resemble what a human would see in a museum on Earth. All the humans who have observed the small number of exhibits that are here, have been quite amazed by their significance. Let's begin by checking out the smaller exhibits on the way to the larger ones in the back.

Here is an original telescope made in 1608 by Hans Lippershey of Zeeland Netherlands. We can't say if this is the first one he created, but it is definitely one of his first. It has a power of three.

James Watt's first steam engine is also here and an attempt to get Newcomb's engine failed.

Over here is a Lee Deforest vacuum tube -- nothing to do with YouTube by the way.

This early television set right here was designed by Philo Farnsworth.

A cat's whisker radio developed by Indian scientist Jagadish Chandra Bose is over here.

This little item is a light bulb stolen from Joseph Swan's collection. Thomas Edison was later to acquire the patent on this light bulb and improve on it.

Many hundreds of years ago, another remarkable invention was created. It's called the 'printing press'. We knew instantly that this would have an enormous influence on human progress. Our curiosity was so intense we decided to get one. Not steal one, but buy it from a printing press manufacturer.

And here it is right here, an original printing press bought from Gutenberg himself. It was one of the latest models and is still in original working order. If you would like to print something with it, go ahead. We always let humans toy around with one of their inventions. From what I know, it makes you human visitors feel a bit more welcome. There are not many things in this museum, but what we do have is fairly significant.

Let me take you through this other door into this very large room.

Awww . . . There she is. What I am pointing out to you is one of the most historically significant sail ships in human history. This is Christopher Columbus' Santa Maria ship, which he discovered the New World with. The official history is that Columbus had to strip the ship because it ran aground, but that is only partially true. In fact, as they began to strip the ship a storm emerged, and they had to abandon it and never came back. Was that an opportunity for us to grab it and bring it home? You betcha!

Let's get a bit closer. As you can see, it's still in good condition after a bit of restoration but not enough to alter its historic importance.

We have two other ships that I'm sure you'll be interested in. Just a bit farther from the Santa Maria is another important ship. Leif Ericson used this Viking ship when he discovered North America while visiting Newfoundland. Buy the time he returned to Greenland it was not in good condition, and his crew abandoned it just north of their colony. After this happened, we kept a very close eye on it and when it became apparent that they had completely lost interest in it, a space shuttle was brought down and snatched it. Yes this is the actual, genuine ship that was the first to arrive in America from Europe.

As interesting as these two ships are, I have a little surprise for you next. Just behind the Viking ship is another ship that most humans have never heard of. Up until now, there have been both theories and postulations as to whether the Chinese people ever travelled to North America in ancient times. There have been books written about it; some research has suggested this might have been true, but no hard scientific evidence exists.

The ship we are presently viewing is *the* Chinese ship that first visited North America in 495 A.D. and landed on Vancouver Island in what is now the nation of Canada. I'd like to inform all humans that visit our museum that it was the Buddhist missionary, Hui Shen, who discovered America when he landed at a place he called Fusang. All those other events you might have heard about -- of Chinese explorers visiting that continent in other centuries -- have never happened. This is the only incident of the Chinese actually visiting North America.

We kept an eye on this entire trip and found his portrayal of this place fascinating. The description of what he saw was written in a document referred to as the ***Book of Liang*** by Yao Silian. He said the land was rich in copper with traces of gold and silver but no iron. The people he encountered lived in civilized communities. They had managed to produce and manufacture paper for writing and cloth for robes and clothing. Numerous houses and cabins dotted the countryside. They had built a well-managed agricultural community, which included raising deer for meat and milk and cheese production.

One of the things that has caused confusion all these years and has sown doubts as to whether this place in Vancouver Island really was the place the Chinese landed on, was a reference to the native peoples riding on horseback. As is well known, native peoples in the Americas at the time did not have horses. We observed the actual landing and subsequent diplomatic introductions and saw no horses whatsoever in that land. So why is there a reference to horses in the Book of Liang?

We can only say that this Book of Liang was written about 150 years after the events of this discovery and some things do become exaggerated over time. Maybe those

Chinese people who wrote the Book of Liang thought it inconceivable that horses couldn't exist anywhere and just assumed the people of Fusang had them.

What Hui Shen saw was a well-governed and law-abiding citizenry with no army or military defense forces. These people had no religion, but Hui Shen did manage to convert a few to his religion of Buddhism.

How did we obtain this ship? An opportunity arose when the owner decided to sell it, and we simply offered him the highest bid.

PART 3: 20TH CENTURY INCIDENTS

Let's leave this exhibit area and enter this other room. This is a special area where all the incidents -- or I should say most incidents -- of both the 20th and 21st centuries we were involved with, will be discussed and revealed.

Let's begin with UFOs. Tales of Unidentified Flying Objects began in the 19th century. That century saw the development of airships by the major powers of the time. Most of these 'unidentified' sightings were human's own airships because that is what people at the time were familiar with. It had nothing to do with us and was the result of fanciful thinking by creative humans.

The real sightings of our vessels appeared much later, sometime after the Second World War. This was a consequence of errors made by pilots and/or captains who were not briefed by our expedition management in how to fly through Earth's airspace.

Let me give you an example. You are already familiar with the term 'flying saucer', which began with the observation of flying disks by Kenneth Arnold in the state of Washington. Those disks were actually garbage that one of our large cruisers dumped by hovering 80 miles above that state. At the time, the Americans were not able to see us on their radar since we had technology that was impenetrable. The garbage they saw were very light-shaped disks that floated down into the atmosphere. It was rather embarrassing for the captain of that cruiser since he wasn't aware that one of his crewmembers had discarded this garbage by mistake.

While he was observing the area (using the typical reconnaissance technology utilized on every spaceship and shuttle), he noticed this garbage and assumed these strange flying objects were caused by unusual human technology that he wasn't aware of. He was so involved in analyzing what was going on, he almost sent a report to the other cruisers in orbit around Earth about his observations when someone finally got around to telling him the truth. So for two brief hours or so, both you humans and us thought we were observing unidentified flying objects. Of course, these objects continued to become part of Earth culture and folklore, but the incident was a blunder on our part.

As technology continued to advance on Earth, we didn't adjust our thinking fast enough in determining how capable humans were when analyzing strange phenomenon for the first time. In the past, humans used a religious rationale to explain our blunders. Not in the 20th century, the assumptions this time were visits from strange beings from another world. We were caught a few times in the 1950s and 60s until we smartened up a bit. But it was too late. Virtually anything that was not readily understandable and was flying in your skies became a flying saucer or UFO even if its origins were from Earth.

One of the most remarkable occurrences was Roswell.

ROSWELL - THE REAL . . . REAL STORY!

Before I begin this historic event, I have an admission to make. We aliens do have pornography. If you are sensitive to this sort of thing, then you might consider skipping this section. I don't wish to offend anyone. Also, if you are underage, and honest, then please apologize to your parents if inserting this information into this book offends them. I want to be perfectly clear here; I am not going to illustrate or demonstrate anything of an actual pornographic nature. And I will only explain this subject in a very scientific and non-demonstrative way. Be careful when you read the following section, because I am deadly serious of what I'm about to say and nothing about it is humorous. I'm going to explain in grim detail about what constitutes sex in our society.

We don't have penises but have exactly 1023 nano-filaments protruding from our heads. When sexually excited, these probes become stiff. How do we become excited since there is no opposite sex?

Consuming a certain type of cell -- that are grown in deep underground caves -- in a certain way causes us to become sexually agitated. The only way of describing this satisfaction is that it feels similar to the sexual pleasure you humans get when males and females copulate. To enjoy this sexual pleasure, and become pregnant, we consume those cells through those filaments on our head, millions at a time. Similar to your sperm and egg cells, these cells are important for reproducing. This biology evolved millions of years ago throughout our evolutionary history.

So that's the sexual part; what about the pornography part? The closest comparison I can make to describe what pornography is in terms that humans can understand is this: On Earth, when a male admires nude female photos, he becomes sexually excited while enjoying the beauty of the female subject. On other occasions, he might perform a particular sexual act of which we won't go into detail here. When the sexual stimulation only is desired (without the reproduction part it's called pornography), a different type of cell is sprayed on those same filaments. The pornographic part of our sexual experience is consuming artificial cells that have been fabricated for the express purpose of sexually stimulating those follicles without making us pregnant.

These cells can only be manufactured in certain star systems that have a unique spectral distribution, which you would call red giants, and have a specific gravitational constant at a certain distance. They are also subjected to an intense bombardment of cosmic radiation. This is too complicated to explain in this book, and if I was to translate all the theory involve in the explanation, it would be about 100 pages long and would require a diverse background in tri-vaginsperm-trans-mathematics (this is the approximate translation from the Regintian language). Please realize that I am being very serious with all these explanations even if you think it's humorous. It definitely is not humorous for us.

Because we are exploring Earth, natural cell consumption is not allowed for reproducing since becoming pregnant would distract us from our mission in this system. So the manufactured cells are imported as a substitution.

The morality of this consumption on our part is considered at about the same moral level as human pornography. When we do it, it is discreet; and if it's done in the presence of other people, then they are usually like minded so as to not be impolite to people who deplore it.

By now you're probably wondering, *what does all this have to do with Roswell?* It all began when someone attempted to deliver this 'pornography' to the explorers on Earth in a transportation cruiser directly from the star system where those cells were fabricated. When the cruiser proceeded into orbit around Earth, about 100 of our people stationed in and around your planet decided to go up to the ship and welcome it -- so much for politeness to people

124

who deplore pornography. It was a party type atmosphere (at least a Regintian party type atmosphere) and that cruiser's captain, who was the only crewmember, was unprepared to meet those small shuttlecraft since it was a cargo ship designed to accept a minimal crew.

Needless to say, the captain lost complete control of the ship because of the aggressive way the visitor's shuttlecraft were surrounding his, and this caused him to crash land near Roswell along with all the pornographic cargo. The crash wasn't a big explosion or anything like that. It was merely a ditching and didn't cause any loss of life. The captain immediately examined the cruiser for damage and since it was somewhat minimal, figured it would take about an hour to fix.

There was a little problem though. Even though he landed in an area that was devoid of human life and had a desert like appearance, it wasn't too long before humans arrived. Because the captain hadn't planned to meet Earthlings, he had to use projection technology to make himself look human, as opposed to a proper cloned person or android. He opened the door, left the cruiser, and waved to the people who had come to investigate him. He had them fooled somewhat, until one of the humans offered him a drink of water. He accepted the bottle and not exactly knowing what to do with it, because of his inexperience with humans, accidentally sprayed himself near his face. To make matters worse, he walked through high intensity radio waves near a broadcast antenna that was on a truck the humans had brought, which caused him to become more exposed.

After all these events happened, I interviewed this person and recorded it. He is assigned the name of Tejago for earth-speak purposes.

Here is the video.

"So, what happened when your projection imaging stopped functioning after being sprayed with water and bombarded with radio waves?"

"The first thing I did was try to communicate in their own language to calm things down. Then I noticed I had a defective translation device, which forced me to use a combination of sign language and drawings to communicate. It was frightening for both of us. They were scared has hell thinking I might hurt them, and I was also scared."

"How did you indicate to them you were harmless?"

"I held up two of my appendages as if I were under arrest. I had seen this practice in a human movie once when law enforcers apprehend bad people. That seemed to ease them a bit. Even though I could escape rather easily if I used some form of violent behavior, my plan was to depart as quickly as possible without doing any harm. It wasn't too long before these soldiers took me away in that truck and held me in a huge room with armed guards just about everywhere. Although my translator wasn't functioning, I knew enough English as far as writing skills were concerned that I was able to communicate reasonably well."

"What happened next?"

"A person of high rank within their armed forces entered the room surrounded by two guards. From what I know of humans, he had a friendly look on his face. I'm sure my friendly face was incomprehensible to him. There was a table between the two of us. He motioned for me to sit near it. Since we really don't sit on chairs, I moved toward it and did my usual squatting. He approached the opposite side of the table and sat down in a chair. I motioned to him with my appendage (using it as an arm) that I could communicate with him by writing. He understood and gave me a piece of paper and a pen. This is what I wrote on it.

" 'Hello, my name is Tejago. I don't speak English but can read and write it in a simple context.'

"He seemed impressed, so this is what he wrote.

" 'Hello, my name is Bert, and I am in charge of this facility here. I would like to know where you come from, and what you want.'

"At this point, I had to be careful and not give away our plans about studying Earth. So I responded, 'I was traveling from a distant star to another star close to here but became lost as my spaceship was hit by a meteor, and I landed here.' "

"Did you think he believed you?"

"What could I do? I was just ad-libbing it at the moment: not exactly sure what to say. Bert continued with his interrogation.

" 'What are you going to do if we let you go?'

"I wrote, 'I will continue with my trip to that neighboring star system.'

" 'Why are you going there, and will this knowledge of Earth affect your plans or the plans of your people?'

"I had to be very careful here since I knew to a certain extent that this person, and the beings he represented, could be quite paranoid. So I lied to him and responded:

" 'We've known about Earth for years and years, and your presence here means absolutely nothing to us since the vast majority of star systems have huge amounts of intelligent life. This is so common throughout the galaxy that I'll probably forget about you by the time I reach that other star system I was referring to.' His mannerisms, as far as I could tell, appeared somewhat relieved. Now I wrote:

" 'I am most pleased to meet you. I 'd like to know when I can leave here.'

"He thought for a moment and wrote: 'I can't say when we will allow you to leave as we want to be sure about our safety.'

"I wrote: 'You must realize that unless I get back to my travel route right away, my people will come and get me out. We are very powerful and would have no trouble destroying the surrounding area. But we are not the type of beings who harm anyone or anything. The best thing for you would be to let me go, and I can assure you nothing will happen to your planet since it has no value to us.'

"Of course I was lying like a rug as humans would say. I yearned to leave here as soon as possible, and I thought both reassuring him and scaring him would do the trick.

" 'I will pass your request on to my superiors. Is there anything I can do for you to make you feel more comfortable.'

"I was silent for a few moments, and then I wrote: 'I'd want you to know, there are two kinds of people who could rescue me. The first are diplomats, who will quite nicely negotiate with you to let me go. The second are non-diplomats, people whom you humans would call businessmen. They are not so nice. There will be no negotiating with them, and please realize that just as our technology is very advanced -- we do travel around the galaxy -- our weapons are also very powerful.'

"If I could smile like a human, I would have been smiling right then. He wrote, 'I'll see what I can do.'

"Was this the only person you communicated with? Were there any other people involved?"

"He left the room for about an hour and returned with two other people. These people went through the same routine and more or less asked the same questions as far as I could tell. Unfortunately, my knowledge of humanity was a little too basic, and I didn't seem to be getting anywhere. I had studied a

128

certain amount about earthlings on the way over to this system and was surprised by one thing -- gambling! Gambling is considered a pastime and a game on our world, and there is no money involved. It is highly mathematical and statistical. A card game similar to poker is far too simple for us even from a psychological point of view."

"What are you getting at here Tejago?"

"As I was trying to communicate with these people, they gave me the impression that they were attempting to manipulate me to go along with them. Keeping me prisoner while not admitting it and trying to extract everything I know about our species and place of origin. I was an expert in the art of bluffing and wondered if they were bluffing me, or could I bluff them? I wrote something down on the paper that totally startled them: 'Do you people know how to play poker?'

"Bert had a confused look on his face. He wrote, 'What do you know about poker and why are you asking?' The so-called 'friendly' mood of this meeting changed to a bewildered state of mind. It now became a matter of skilful negotiation, where there were elements of both bluffing and deception. I just about had the perfect poker face. There was no way these human's could look at me and try to interpret my intentions through any sort of body language I might display; I was totally alien to them. If anything, I was able to scrutinize them -- being more familiar with human physiology -- and read the looks on their faces with ease. Bert was frowning slightly probably wondering if he was in any kind of trouble. One of his assistants had an 'Oh shit' look on his face. The other person in the room looked like he was about to cry. I still had to be careful though; if anyone panicked, things could become unpredictable.

"I yearned to get out of there as soon as possible, but do it gently. In general, our species has about ten times the strength of humans, and I also had a powerful weapon located in my body, which they couldn't have known about since they do not know anything about my physiology. My gambling instincts advised me to continue to emphasize that idea about 'business associates' rescuing me. So I wrote: 'Recall those powerful and possibly violent business people that might come and rescue me, the longer you wait in detaining my release, the greater the chance of annoying them. Detaining me in this manner might be injurious to your health, and unless you are excellent poker players, you're placing yourself in a position of shall we say . . . ill-treatment?'

"At this point, even I was amazed at my own cunning. After all, I've had no experience whatsoever dealing with humans yet was enjoying myself in this 'crapshoot'. Was I making any sense to them with this little 'bluff'? I continued to explore that possibility using that big 'stick', while in the next instant I presented them with a 'carrot': 'If you can let me go now, I'll allow you to board our spacecraft so that you can glimpse our alien technology.' My plan was to entice these specific humans only and not their entire infrastructure, just these three people. This negotiation went on and on, with me deflecting question after question while trying to be evasive. At the end of the day, they had to go to sleep and there I was, squatting in this room for an additional ten hours before anyone reappeared.

"That next morning, Bert returned to the room and wrote, 'I was able to persuade our management to let you go since you are allowing us to view the inside of your spaceship assuming you will allow these two men in it. One of them will have a movie camera, and the other will have a regular camera.' He pointed to the two men.

"I wrote down, 'I agree with this deal.' I did not intend to allow this to happen and as we walked out of the building, my head was twirling with ways of avoiding this agreement. Bert, his two 'camera' colleagues and three armed guards, were the only people seen on our way to my ship. The building and surrounding areas were completely devoid of humans. Bert pointed to a vehicle indicating the method of transporting us to my spaceship. I 'climbed' aboard the vehicle and traveled for about five minutes until we arrived at the destination. It didn't appear to have been tampered with other than a few scar marks and dirt over it.

"Now I had to be careful. I was sure the ship could fly but also knew it needed to be flown slower since the repairs were not up to-date. I searched around and noticed that almost every airplane in this military airport had a pilot standing near its cockpit ready to board and take-off. There were also airplanes already flying in the air."

"So what was your plan Tejago?"

"I allowed the two cameramen to take numerous pictures inside the ship, then secretly destroyed the pictures, gave the cameras back to Bert, and then he issued them with new ones for the flight session. After all that was done, my ship departed and I fooled my two passengers into believing they were flying in a predetermined route, which I had previously agreed to, by showing them bogus displays as the ship rose vertically."

"Did you check to see if your 'pornographic cargo' was intact."

"I did check and surprisingly it was nowhere to be found."

"What could possibly have happened to it?"

"Using the ship's translator, I turned to these 'companions' and asked them where the cargo could have gone. Their answer was 'What cargo?' I explained to them that I had a biological cargo comprised of cellular structures that were contained in a huge cylinder. They contacted Bert and explained to him my concern. His response was, 'You mean that object we saw falling from your ship on its way down here was a cylinder of alien cell structures?'

"I was horrified. Not only was this precious cargo missing, but what havoc could it have caused when it crash landed? I was determined to get that cargo back no matter what. This time I spoke to him directly, 'Bert, do you know where this cargo is?'

" 'I believe it fell near a place called Roswell, but we haven't been able to locate it.' The on-board android controller automatically did a quick scan near that town attempting to locate it. The cargo didn't appear to be anywhere near it, so the scanning continued in the surrounding areas and then in the surrounding states. It took awhile, but eventually the scanner detected the cargo in what appeared to be warehouses in a place that would later be referred to as AREA 51.

"So Tejago, why didn't Bert know where they were?"

"I have to admit I was perplexed. He did claim to be in charge of the facility after all. No point in wasting any more time, I increased my altitude in an upward direction. My quick vertical acceleration startled the aircraft that were already flying above me judging by the translated conversations from their radio communications.

"There was another little problem for these fighters. Their missiles were designed to detect targets based on infrared energy, but there was none emanating from my ship. Even at a slow speed, my ship was able to zip past the propeller driven fighters in very little time. In the meantime, my two human colleagues were taking pictures of the fictitious views that were being displayed on the inside panels.

"Another remarkable technology that humans haven't invented yet was the ability to shield against accelerating forces, so when my ship gathered speed no one on board could feel it. It was now a matter of attaining a velocity that was beyond the capability of any human aircraft, and then landing far away in a park in the same state. When we arrived at the landing area, the two humans thought they had landed back in the same military airport. I explained to them, 'Your commanding officer directed me to land near those trees close to that building at this airport.'

"When they left my ship, they saw those trees and for a brief instance were fooled into believing they were back at their base. By then, the door to my craft was closed, and off I went. There was a paved road about a mile away, so I knew they would be safe and would have no problem finding their way back."

"So what happened to all the pictures they took?"

"They were blacked out by having one of the android controls in my ship emit a brief split second burst of radiation at these cameras, which destroyed the film."

"So tell me how you retrieved the cargo."

"I flew up to about 100 miles where I knew I couldn't be detected and hovered over the AREA 51 warehouses containing my cargo. I sent a small undetectable probe down into the suspected warehouse where the cargo was supposed to be, and yes there it was, in a constantly guarded room. There were people entering the room, and they were wearing special garments that would supposedly protect them from anything our cells might do to them. They weren't aware that those particular cells were completely harmless to them. If anything, Earth biological life was dangerous to those cells. Virtually any Earth type DNA or RNA molecular structures could easily destroy them.

"This room and building, even though they couldn't detect my spy probe, had very tough security surrounding it, and I knew it was impossible to retrieve that cylinder without forcing myself in and causing a lot of damage, injury, and even death. I had to have an ingenious way of getting that stuff back without causing a ruckus. So I headed straight back to our HQ on the Lunar-Base and after a big explanation of what happened -- which included a criticism of the staff that originally went up to welcome me -- a plan was devised which would include penetrating that Area 51 building with a couple of cloned agents. I was excluded from this cloning process because I wasn't really trained for it and had no desire to go through that course of action.

"Our people were to observe this whole rescue plan in real time on a display screen, whether they were on the moon or located on Earth in our hidden Monitoring Stations. Such was the intense curiosity of those porno cells."

"So what was your purpose?"

"My purpose was to fly a very small stealth shuttle and haul the cylinder out of the area after my cloned colleagues grabbed it and hustled it out of the building. When the rescue plan went into effect, they eventually penetrated the base and entered the building without too much difficulty, but trying to get into the specific warehouse inside that building was a bit more difficult. We concluded that we had to destroy the cells since there was no way of retrieving them. This caused an absolute uproar amongst our people who were listening and watching the event unfold. But the uproar lasted a mere 1/2 second."

(We Regintians compute, think and come to conclusions far faster than humans -- Appleton.)

"So how were you going to destroy them?"

"The solution was to broadcast certain destructive signals from a special transmitter. Since most biology on Reginta communicates in the same way, the cells in these cylinders would be sent a specific signal and would self-destruct.

This is Appleton again.

Sorry to interrupt my replay of Tejago's interrogation, but I need to explain a few things here. I must warn you; this is a very geeky explanation of what's going on.

Since we are recollecting these 20th century events, it is most important to expose this for the record (I wouldn't dare put the following documentation in a 'novel' for example). If you are bored by geekation (I think that's the correct word) then please ignore the following paragraphs.

How does this remote cell destruction work? I have to specifically explain how the sexual part works again (again my apologies to parents if your kids happened to be reading this book since it's not officially x-rated). While these pornographic details might be offensive to some, it should make a computer geek's day after reading this.

Remember when I mentioned that we have exactly 1023 follicles on our head. This of course is 3FF in hexadecimal notation and 11 1111 1111 in binary notation.

What's the significance of all of this? Computer and math people will understand the concept of the weight of a digit in a binary number.

For example: 1 has a value of 1, 11 has a value of 3, 111 has a value of 7, 1111 has a value of 15.

You software people know what I mean. Each 'porno cell' (if I may call them that) has an official value or weight. A cell with a weight of 7 will attempt to occupy 3 follicles while a cell with a value of 127 or 1111111 will try to occupy 7 follicles. When we spray these cells onto our skulls, they enter those follicles as per the above parameters and then the sexual enjoyment happens.

By the way, all these cells are capable of receiving radio waves, just as we are. When they receive human radio waves, it makes no sense and all they hear is noise. When they receive binary encoded radio waves with the correct parameters, they hear genuine communication.

To destroy these cells by radio waves we normally aim an extremely powerful antenna at them from about 300 meters, and since we're competing with all the human radio noise down there, we have to make sure our self destruct symbols are 'heard' by the cells. These signals are streamed 'quadary' data (four voltage levels rather than two) that the cells decode into the correct 'weights'.

Now back to Tejago's interrogation.

"Since my colleagues wouldn't be removing the cylinders anymore, we now needed to aim powerful radio waves at them."

"I wonder whose job that was going to be?"

"You guessed right Appleton. Since I was the guy in the shuttle, it was my job to aim and fire. I had to get down to Area 51 quickly and avoid any potential anti-aircraft fire or fighters sent out to pursue me. We have a lot of fancy technology on our side, and I planned to use as much of it as possible. The stealth shield would definitely be on when penetrating that perimeter. Blasting those radio waves for one second at the cell cylinder was the next step. Grabbing my colleagues and then hightailing it out of there was next. Later on, a probe would descend to investigate whether I had destroyed the cells."

"So what happened?"

"Everything went fine at first. My shuttle descended in the middle of the night, and no one saw it as far as we know. Their radar didn't pick up my

profile. When I got near the warehouse, the security people spotted my shuttle, and you could observe them scrambling about. The speed I was traveling at was in my favor, and they only saw me for about 10 seconds during which time I fired my radio waves, grabbed my colleagues, and rapidly went back to outer space. The operation looked successful. But when we sent our confirmation probe down in the next hour, we discovered that the cylinder had been removed. We sent more probes down, but they could not locate the cylinder. What a disaster that was."

"Did the humans move them before or after you bombarded them with radio waves and were the cells dead or alive, and where was the cylinder?"

"Good questions, but I had an idea; why don't I go down there -- surrounded with a shield in case someone would fire a weapon at me -- and abduct a human and demand to know where they put the cells. My superiors thought I was crazy. So I proposed asking for Bert, the person we had made contact with before. They thought our credibility with Bert had been reduced since I lied to him when escaping from the Roswell area. Someone asked me why didn't I interrogate Bert when he was on board the spaceship with those two photographers. Right in the middle of this heated discussion, I took the position of accusing my superiors of second guessing me."

"So where could Bert be at the present time?"

"I figured he could be in one of two places, still at Roswell, or transferred over to Area 51. Two swarms of 'hound dog' nanobots (using earth-speak here) would be sent down to sniff out his DNA, as if we had sent a pack of hound dogs to locate him. Our nanobots would do a better job, and be much faster. So down they went and Bert was found in about a day."

"Where was he?"

"He was in Area 51. I went down with a cloned colleague in case we needed a human form. The plan was for me to meet with Bert personally and try to find out where our cells were. We would do that in several ways. One was to ask him, or get him to find out from his colleagues. The other way was to send down another swarm of nanobots, which would check all of the surrounding areas where Bert was stationed that we hadn't searched before."

"So what happened?"

"We landed right in the middle of a parking lot near a building where Bert was located, at about 8 PM. As soon as we landed, all radar and stealth cloaking shields were deactivated. Then Bert was called on the standard frequencies of their radio communications equipment. You could tell we were causing a commotion as all kinds of armed personnel were scrambling around and surrounding our shuttle. The weapons shield was still on, so we were not too concerned about intentional or unintentional gunfire.

"I called Bert on the radio and waited. Finally, on the same frequency, he answered back. 'This is Bert, am I speaking with Tejago?'

" 'Yes this is me. Would you know where that cylinder I mentioned last time I met you, is located?' There was a bit of silence as if Bert wasn't too sure what to say.

" 'I'm not sure where it is, and the people here don't know what you're talking about.' As he was mentioning this, we were already receiving signals from our probes and something amazing was indicated. Not only did the probes indicate where it was, but we had landed right on top of it. Just below our shuttle underneath the parking lot was a basement area, and from what our sensors were reporting, our cylinder was right there and still contained the cells.

"Then I had an idea; since we were right on top of the cells, maybe they could be retrieved rather than destroyed. We immediately began to drill a hole into the parking lot ground while I attempted to distract Bert and his associates long enough to prevent them from interfering.

"It was obvious from Bert's chatter that he was lying, and this was causing a beneficial delay for us since he had to spend time with his colleagues sorting the facts out while the drilling continued. This drilling wasn't easy and that's because it had to be done quickly before the humans could prevent it. The first hole was small, and I intended to pump in a special gas that would put to sleep any humans that might be down there. The next thing would be to send a probe down to search for problems that could obstruct us before we drilled a bigger hole. With a bit of luck the probe would indicate if there were any humans sleeping down there that could be hurt by the next drilling phase.

"That first hole was drilled quickly, the gas was pumped in, and then the spy probes where sent down. We didn't notice any humans lying around at all, at least not around the shuttle area. When the big drilling got under way -- which was a bit noisier -- Bert demanded to talk. 'What's going on? My people are telling me you are destroying the pavement underneath you.'

" 'One moment Bert while I check with my colleague to find out what he is doing.'

"That was another delaying tactic to buy more time. 'Bert, from what he tells me the cylinder is directly underneath us, and he wants to confirm if that's true.'

" 'I honestly doubt that Tejago. If you can stop that drilling, I'll go down there and see for myself if your cylinder is there.'

"I said, 'Sure, I can do that.' It just so happened that the drilling was finished. Now we had to get down

139

there quickly to retrieve the cylinder. That was my job since I was physically stronger than my partner who had the human clone. My plan was to roam around while continuing to talk with Bert (don't forget I use radio waves to communicate), and Bert would still think I was in the shuttle.

"So we rushed out of the shuttle, went down the hole, and upon getting there noticed the cylinder in relatively good shape. It didn't appear to have been tampered with, so I approached it and was just about to grab it, when I noticed a human in an oxygen mask. Then I see another and another. They were all aiming weapons at us.

"I ask my partner, 'What do you think we should do now?'

"His response, 'Why are you asking me; you're the experienced one here having to deal with Bert and some of those other humans.' Just to appear less aggressive to these soldiers who were pointing weapons at me, I took two of my appendages off the cylinder and stuck them in the air.

"Then I called Bert, 'Bert, there are people down here which I think might be holding weapons at us, can you confirm this?'

"Bert's response, 'Where are you?'

" 'I'm in an underground warehouse.'

" 'How did you get down there?'

" 'I drilled a hole into the ground which also penetrated the ceiling in this warehouse. I want that cylinder now Bert, as those business people I mentioned before, are expecting delivery of this in a few days. You wouldn't want to get those people upset would you?' I was betting on the fact that Bert would still remember my concerns about these 'business people' from the last time he heard about it. This would hopefully persuade him into letting the cylinder and us go.

" 'I'm afraid that before we can let this container go, we would like to ask you a few more questions.'

"More questions? Didn't this guy asked enough last time we met? 'Ok go ahead.'

" 'We want to know what's in there, and why can't we examine it?'

" 'As I said before, this is a shipment of biological cellular material for a customer that is far away from your solar system, and they will be very upset if we don't deliver this. You definitely do not want these people showing up in your neighborhood. Let's just say they are not the friendly type.'

" 'My associates have confirmed that those people down there are guards, and they are trying to remove other people that have passed out because of the gas you released into that area,' said Bert.

" 'Don't worry about that gas; it's harmless. As for those weapons their aiming at us, could you kindly tell them to put them away as we have weapons that are vastly superior, and believe me you do not want us to use them against your people.' This was stretching the truth of course. But wasn't Bert also stretching it when he mentioned the guards were trying to remove sleeping bodies? As I mentioned before, I never saw any.

"Yes, we do have superior weapons, and there was a shield surrounding me. It was very basic and not something that would be used to protect ourselves against human firepower, because we weren't too sure how effective it would be against their weapons. Would their weapons penetrate our weaker shields because of the close range? If those guards had been farther away, I would have felt more confident that they couldn't do us any harm.

" 'Hello, this is Bert's commanding officer, Colonel Parkerson.'

"At this point my partner said, 'I wonder who this is; his voice sounds tense.' I went back up into the shuttle.

"The colonel continued, 'Please forgive us for appearing so aggressive, but you have to realize that we don't deal with life forms like you every day, and we do have to protect ourselves against something which we do not know anything about. The last time we agreed on something, all we got in return was blank film.'

"My response was, 'I don't know anything about that. If your film was blank, it definitely wasn't our fault and could have been caused by the unusual environment in our ship, and your camera technology probably didn't take it into account. So maybe that's why it was defective.' That was another pack of lies on my part. If lies worked the last time, maybe they'll work this time as well.

" 'I'll tell you what, we'll let you go, but first I want to send my cameramen into your craft, take pictures, then leave, and then we'll examine the film to make sure it hasn't been tampered with or become defective. After that you are free to go with all your belongings.'

"I looked at my partner and asked him what he thought. 'Do we really care whether they have photos of the inside of our shuttle?' I said.

" 'The problem is that officially humans are not supposed to know of our existence. This would be a major exposure and not like the other incidences when we had plausible deniability.'

" 'How can we alter this exposure?'

" 'I have an idea; every time they snap a picture let's fire in photons of images of obscure Earth technology that we have on file. Then when they scrutinize their film to check for overexposure, they'll see objects and imagine they'll have legitimate photos of our spaceship, where they'll actually have Earth type photos. When they figure out later they've been had again, it will be too late.'

" 'Ok let's go with this plan.'

"I called the colonel and said, 'I agree with your offer. Send your people over right now.'

" 'Thank you; I will send two people over with their cameras, and they will not have any weapons.'

The two photographers emerged out of a nearby building and strode over to our shuttle. They both wore gas masks and paused just outside the door. As I opened it, they rushed up a slight incline and entered. The cameras they used had these annoying flashbulbs when they took pictures. Every time a picture was taken, they had to replace the bulb which slowed own the whole process. While this was happening, I manipulated certain controls that would send small flying nanobots up to the camera lens. A swarm of these would hover in front of the lens so when the camera operator pressed the shutter, the nanobots automatically sent in photonic patterns of what we wanted them to see. What was imprinted on their film were technical pictures of vacuum tubes, which was the most advanced electronic technology of the day. After they left, I hauled in the cylinder and immediately took off before anyone found out what happened. Now it was up to the exploration management to verify that stupid incidences like this never happened again.

"What would humans say if they were in my place? . . . Whew!"

That was the Tejago interview. We still had another problem. Knowing the memories of those humans -- who observed both a Regintian and a spaceship first hand -- couldn't be wiped out, we wondered if and how this information would be disseminated around Earth.

It didn't take too long before the story appeared in the Roswell Daily Record newspaper on July 8, 1947. What was remarkable about it was the U.S. military attitude. They denied it and claimed it was just a radar-tracking balloon.

Later in 1994, the U.S. Air Force stated it was an attempt to detect long distance sound waves from the Soviet Union referred to as project Mogul. The US government position was a stroke of luck for us. They wanted to keep this as quiet as we did.

Just in case you were wondering, we were never in communication with any government on Earth even though UFO conspiracy theorists alleged the opposite. No matter how quiet the U.S. government and we Regintians wanted this, it became a very long lasting and popular story all over the world.

CROP CIRCLES

Another controversy we began was something called crop circles. I'm dragging Tasall back in and he will quickly explain this one.

The Crop circle phenomenon inadvertently began when we landed one of our spaceships by mistake in a farmer's field in Tully Australia in 1966. That spaceship was surveying a swamp area and didn't realize there was a human observing it nearby. Our vessel was slightly submerged and would occasionally have to rise up and down to properly survey the area. We were aware at the time of deforming the landscape but never considered that humans would find these patterns since they would eventually erode away with time.

A farmer nearby spotted us, went to get his camera, and then took a picture of one of these deformations. From that moment on, our management forbade anyone to go down in any spacecraft during the day and if we were ever to land, our instructions were to do so in an area that would leave no detectable pattern. From then on, all evidence left behind was to be wiped out.

If anything, we thought society as a whole would have dismissed this farmer as a prankster. That wasn't a very good prediction. The area eventually attracted a large gathering of news people and officials, and even the Royal Australian Air force became involved.

It didn't end there. A couple of pranksters named Bower and Chorley in the United Kingdom imitated the idea, and they began making artificial patterns all over the UK. This scheme spread and spread with the help of other pranksters, and now these observations have become a bona fide pseudoscience.

And it all began with this one pattern in Australia.

Ok Appleton, Can I go now?

Yes Tasall.

You can go. Just say good-bye to the Earthling. . .

Without fail, every time I ask him to say goodbye to you earthlings when you visit here, he takes off without doing it.

THE ALIEN AUTOPSY

This next incident is one of the weirdest situations I can think of considering we managed to fool just about anyone who thought they knew of our visits to Earth. During the 1970s and '80s, there were thousands of claims of UFO observations, abductions, and other events, no doubt caused by the Roswell occurrence. Even though humans have probably observed us in this century more than in any other, the amount of times it has actually happened can be counted on one human hand (well maybe two); yet claims of UFO sightings number in the thousands.

What was going on here? One of our historians derived a theory that humans are replacing belief in religion with belief in strange physical phenomena. As humans become less susceptible to explanations involving spiritual intervention, they become more susceptible to out of world and/or mystic rationalizations.

This historian devised an experiment where he would place innocuous events viewable to humans, to observe if they conjured up out of world explanations.

His name is Foduenow, and here is his story.

I arrived on Earth with a colleague to search for a serious UFO believer -- which wasn't hard to do -- to observe them 'observing'. You wouldn't believe how low the standards are that these people use in coming to conclusions about extraterrestrials. As a way of demonstrating this, I waited until this group of people, or informal club, went out on a nightly expedition to a local park reputed to be a producer of unexplained flying phenomena. Despite their enthusiasm, I never saw anything that remotely resembled a UFO. And if there was anyone who knew whether an actual UFO was out that night, it would be me -- I am a Regintian after all.

So one evening I sneaked over to the other side of the park, lit up a few standard 60-watt tungsten light bulbs, and brought them up a hill. On the way up I blinked the lights at about once per second. This flashing lasted about five minutes.

The next day at their meeting, all of the members were adamant they had witnessed a genuine UFO. After that incident, I became even more ambitious to demonstrate the lack of standards these human UFO enthusiasts had. This time my idea was to plant a false alien corpse modeled on a standard picture of these creatures that humans had conjured up over the years.

At first, I was going to let it dangle from a tree or building and let people take pictures of it before removing it. The creature was to be created from Earth animal guts to make it appear genuine, and I also wanted to make sure that it wouldn't find its way into a real lab for the time being. That would occur later when the debunking phase materialized.

As I assembled this 'monstrosity' in one of our Monitoring Stations, an opportunity presented itself when I learned of an English entrepreneur exploring the idea of creating a fake film on an alien autopsy. I thought this person would be ideal for receiving 'real' fake footage. My modus operandi was to impersonate a U.S. military officer and claim to be involved in the UFO cover-ups. I would inform this person that the film I possessed was authentic from 1948 and stolen from U.S. government archives, while it would actually be a fake autopsy of a fake corpse composed of Earth animal tissue. If this person was going to sell a fake alien autopsy film, wouldn't he rather sell one that's 'real' as opposed to one he would conjure up.

We would manufacture the face using actual tissue from Earth animals put together with our own biological techniques using nanobots. To set these people up and fool them, we used an orangutan, altered the face slightly, and removed all the hair to make it appear more alien. Anyone who did an autopsy and used advanced DNA techniques available in 1995 could easily determine this was an orangutan, and not a being from outer space. When I finally made contact, he and his colleagues wholeheartedly accepted my offer.

Now here's the weird part. I initially revealed to him still photographs of these 'aliens', and now I had to produce a film that not only resembled a 1940s vintage but also had to make it appear aged. It was extremely difficult and time consuming, and trickier than I thought. My co-worker and I placed the film in a chamber and subjected it to special nanobots that would pick away at the molecular structure until the film appeared old.

What we didn't realize was that the nanobots had done too good of a job. They had picked away at the film so much that one had to handle it very carefully. Deterioration was practically guaranteed if placed into the proper camera projection device.

Well guess what happened? When I handed the film to those people, they ran it in that device out of sheer curiosity (even though I had warned them) and through various other means totally mishandled the film until there were just a few viewable frames left.

So what did they do? They produced their own film and released it to the FOX network in 1995 in the United States. Later in 2006, they claimed to have faked the film except for a few frames that had not yet deteriorated. But they still declared the aliens authentic.

When I got a chance to review it, I couldn't find any part of the film I gave him anywhere in it. Funny thing is, is that both films are fakes! They tried to fool the public with their fake film, we tried to fool them with our fake film, so who won the foolery competition?

Let's just say that we completely bamboozled those business people, while they did not necessarily

fool all the public. Skeptics are still out there, with most of the public not believing this story.

That was Foduenow.

That was a lesson for us and was the end of his experimentation in human pseudoscience.

BETTY AND BARNEY HILL ABDUCTION

I would now like to switch you back to Farlee.

Good day Earthling, this is Farlee again.

First of all, I want to ask you a question assuming that you are able to speak to me. Appleton usually informs me whether a visiting human is capable of communicating with me but on a few occasions has been wrong. In fact, we've had the odd human visitor who was able to speak but wasn't aware of it for some strange reason. We still haven't been able to figure out why. Please say something just to confirm you are one of the few Earthlings who are able to communicate ...

Well I still don't hear anything from you, so I have to assume that I will be doing all the talking.

The reason I sought to talk with you is to ask you if you knew anything concerning the Barney and Betty Hill incident. I am officially in charge of this case along with other duties here at the museum. I was going to turn you over to our interrogator who works with the law enforcement agency on Reginta. He wants to communicate with every human who visits here. Even though we have read all the possible material ever produced by the Barney and Betty Hill story, we want to make sure that any new information is not missed. That's why every human who visits here is asked to co-operate. The interrogator is now leaving the room since he won't be needed.

Let me continue with this incident.

There are many accounts and UFO testimonials about extraterrestrial encounters. You humans even characterize them by calling them encounters of the 1st, 2nd, and 3rd kinds. I would like to inform you that the vast majority of these sightings and meetings are false: the result of human imagination and/or deceit. I keep

track of these events to document human idiosyncrasies and characteristics.

Many years ago, I stumbled onto a book called *Interrupted Journey*, which was about a so-called abduction of two people, Barney and Betty Hill. After I read it, I classified it as another weird human story since we are the only aliens visiting Earth, and records of us having anything to do with these two people simply don't' exist in our data banks.

That was back in 1965. In 2005, as we continued to acquire more information of UFO abductions, a new member of our documentation team (let's name him Freddyco) scrutinized a lot of this pseudoscience material as a hobby to create a scrapbook of sorts, so he could show people at home when he got back to Reginta.

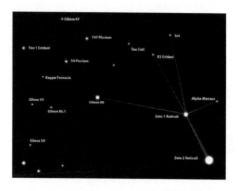

In this material, he came across a star-map from that Barney Hill incident. Freddyco placed this star-map prominently in his scrapbook (by the way, the scrapbook is a three-dimensional projection emitting from a hand-held device). No one took notice of this map until he revealed it to the pilot of a space vessel, and the pilot instantly recognized it.

"How interesting," he told the pilot.

While pointing to various parts of it, the pilot mentioned, "The area indicated by this map is near this solar system, and we always travel through it on our way over here." After a few minutes of idle chatter, they departed and by this time Freddyco was ready to go home to Reginta.

Just before he was about to leave, he dropped by my office at our Lunar-Base to say good-bye. We had a little chat, and I decided to accompany him to the spaceship.

As we approached the ship, Freddyco mentioned what the pilot had told him. That statement struck me, and I wondered how he could recognize the map if it had been 'invented' by one of those two people -- Betty Hill I believe. How could this fantasized illusion be real, if simply fabricated from a dream? What are the chances of an ordinary person being able to dream up a map of a star system from a different viewpoint than Earth, and being reasonably accurate?

After I said goodbye, I visited the pilot and asked him to point out the star-map that Freddyco had in his scrapbook. He placed it on the viewing screen and pointed out that these stars were located on a regular trade route for transport cruisers, and most pilots would observe them on the way to Earth.

So here is the mystery, how could Betty Hill devise this star chart considering humans haven't even travelled to the stars yet. Yes, we were aware of what Earth scientists knew about neighboring star clusters and to a certain extent, they could more or less produce a 3D projection of certain groupings.

So where did this layout come from? Could an astronomer have informed her about this, allowing her to present it as her own? I was determined to scrutinize all the available data to examine it for clues. I reread the book *Interrupted Journey* and the following two paragraphs put me on alert.

The first paragraph:

"It reminded Barney of a huge pancake. Carrying his pistol in his pocket, he stepped away from the vehicle and moved closer to the object. Using the binoculars, Barney claimed to have seen about eight to

153

eleven humanoid figures who were peering out of the craft's windows, seeming to look at him. In unison, all but one figure moved to what appeared to be a panel on the rear wall of the hallway that encircled the front portion of the craft."

The second paragraph:

"Barney had a conscious, continuous recollection of observing the humanoid forms wearing glossy black uniforms and black caps. Red lights on what appeared to be bat-wing fins began to telescope out of the sides of the craft and a long structure descended from the bottom of the craft. The silent craft approached to what Barney estimated was within 50–80 feet overhead and 300 feet away from him."

Two things stand out: the craft's windows in the first paragraph, and the 'Red lights on what appeared to be bat-wing fins began to telescope out of the sides of the craft and a long structure descended from the bottom of the craft' from the second paragraph. We have thousands of different models and variations of spacecraft, and I have to admit I'm not familiar with all of them. I consulted a space vessel expert on our Lunar-base and despite a rather vague description of this particular spacecraft, he was quite sure he knew what they were referring to.

"It's a rare vessel that hasn't been built for at least 10,000 years," he said.

"The average lifespan of a spaceship is about 1000 years. Then it's either replaced with a new vessel and the old one discarded by dumping it in a star where it burns up, or is sold in the used vessel market. It's just like the used car market on Earth. I finished searching our database records, and it produced only one incident indicating a spacecraft similar to this could still be in use."

"Where could it be then?" I said.

"Apparently, this model fell into the hands of one of our explorers -- who happens to be an amateur collector -- whose goal was to restore it but never got around to it. According to our records, it was stolen and vanished for about 20 years. Then it resurfaced when our law enforcement officials arrested the occupants and jailed them for theft."

"Do you realize that when these people vanished with this spacecraft, the time they were gone overlapped the time of that Barney and Betty incident," I said.

"That strikes me as a major coincidence. Maybe you should ask our Lunar-Base law enforcement authorities to check the spacecraft for any insights regarding this story since they usually don't destroy evidence," responded the space vessel expert.

He was right. After all, when you have the ability to travel all over the galaxy, you don't' exactly run out of room to store things, and you don't ever have to throw away anything.

All spacecraft use android technology. This feature allows them to remember every little detail of what the ship did during its lifetime. That means there should be records of what happened during all its voyages -- except those people who were arrested might have erased places that they had visited. We decided to examine the vessel to find out. You never know, one might be able to extract a few clues.

What we were seeking:

Did the craft and its people ever visit New Hampshire?

Did the people who abducted Barney and Betty do something to them?

If the above were true, then what was the reason for doing so?

We pulled the spacecraft out of storage and examined it with a fine-tooth comb (in the Regintian language we actually use the phrase "full tooth-rake" since we don't really use combs). Determining if it ever visited New Hampshire would be easy if there were any remnants of biological material that would have made their way on to it. If the craft landed in New

Hampshire with the doors opening and letting even the slightest amount of air in, then it shouldn't be too much trouble to detect if New Hampshire-like material was in the spacecraft.

Our technology is sensitive enough that even if one molecule unique to New Hampshire appeared on the ship, then the probability of a visit there increased dramatically. If we found many molecules, then it was a sure deal. We couldn't imagine a situation where a lot of molecules from there would just appear without a visit to that area.

Well guess what, on first examination there was no problem sensing these molecules. Our sensors detected a lot of them with most of them related to typical pollens and insect material that are located in the air in most places in New Hampshire.

That takes care of number one. The next step was to interrogate the former controllers of the spacecraft. This wasn't a problem either. We have devices that can read people's minds and since these prisoners already know that, they usually co-operate.

They went to Earth for the same reason Regintian explorers are there. They were curious about human civilization, but there was an additional motive as well. From their point of view, there was enormous potential for trading in life forms or materials from Earth in a black market.

I finally sat down with the two, and they told me their story. Their names are Billson and Joer. Here is a video of this event.

"Billson, at what point did you decide to go to Earth?"

"We have always thought of a black market in Earth products for many years. It wasn't until we acquired that old spacecraft, while we happened to be near the Solar System, that we seriously considered doing it."

"How long did you have the ship before you used it on Earth?"

"We had it for about a year before we felt ready to go. We hired at least another three people to help us out."

"Three people, I didn't know about that. Do the authorities know about it?"

"They do and those people are still at large."

"Do you think they are still trying to operate a black market on Earth?"

"I don't know if they are directly involved right now but let me tell you that if an opportunity opens up, for sure they will do their best to get into the action."

"Let's get back to Barney and Betty. Tell me what happened, how did you come across them?"

"To be quite honest with you, they were about the 18th or 19th humans we had stopped and examined. Two things needed to get done, first acquire something valuable without being caught. That seemed to be easy enough since no one ever found out about our visits to Earth. We could practically do anything we wanted. Many of the things being searched for were ancient Earth artifacts usually found in museums. There is a ready market of eager buyers amongst many different star systems for this sort of thing. The other thing was to bring back humans and sell them as well. This is why we were examining people like Betty and Barney."

"Who would want to buy a human?"

"There are collectors out there who would love to own them just to show them off to their family and friends. They use them as pets but rarely slaves. Some

customers want tall humans, some want fat ones, and some want them a certain color."

"Have you ever captured and sold these humans?"

"Even though we were thieves, we didn't feel right about abducting humans and selling them. Our compromise was to temporarily abduct them, put them to sleep, then extract sperm and eggs cells and any other cellular material we could think off. Later on, we would use this material to grow humans in incubation chambers and sell them, usually completely grown I might add, to those same people who also bought ancient Earth objects."

"So how many of these humans did you grow?"

"We were just beginning to grow our first humans before we were caught for stealing the spaceship. So no humans left our facilities."

"Let me ask you another question. What about those people who are still at large, do they have human cellular material?"

"As I said before, I am not sure what they are doing, but it is highly likely they are still going after human sperm and egg cells. Once you get a small sample of these, you can keep reproducing them without going back to Earth, and then sell these human copies and make money. The problem is that if you keep using the same material over and over again the variety of humans won't be very high, so that would be an incentive to keep abducting humans."

"Well I have to admit I do find that whole idea rather disgusting. Is there anything we can do to find them and see what they are up to?"

"The first thing you have to do is quarantine Earth much better than you have been doing. It's not just these

former acquaintances of mine who want this, there are many more who would love to get in on the black market."

I was finishing off the interrogation and Joer made an offer.

"If I were you guys I would employ Billson's and my experience with Earth and use us to make sure the Earth stays secure from these types of people."

Joer would love to be released no doubt, and we had to seriously consider what he was saying. We had to secure Earth from these people and even though we thought it was safe, you just never knew. Maybe it wouldn't do any harm to consider his offer.

Later, I got together with the Earth expedition management, and we decided to take Joer up on his offer, released him and Billson from imprisonment, and then get more exact details on what they did during their stay here.

After they were released in 2007, I attempted to confirm that what they told me was in fact a black market dealing with human products and biology. The procedure we chose was a systematic analysis of every detail they mentioned, then checking to see if their friends were still on Earth running the black market.

We scheduled a meeting with the local administrators and developed a procedure for monitoring undocumented Regintians that were loose in the area. We had to admit the irony of the situation; all these thousands of years, we've focused only on human development and events, and now we were focusing on our own people. Some of us felt that a black market had existed for centuries. Joer didn't think so but wasn't sure.

Our first strategy was tightening security around Earth and the moon. We assigned a special orbiting spaceship to check for anything suspicious coming into Earth's vicinity. Examining all staff and personal involved in Earth exploration for any previous association in criminal activity was the next step. Everything on our Earth bases, as well as the moon, would be forensically inspected for anything unusual.

It wasn't too long before our security people discovered a lot of suspicious things with Joer confirming them all. The first noticeable item was the constant absence of certain pieces of equipment, while others made an appearance only occasionally.

Another thing we noticed: when these items were referred to in meetings and get-togethers, they would always be in inventory, as if someone was closely monitoring the conversation of certain people, to determine the probability of what equipment should be in inventory by what was being said. Once it got around that an investigation was underway, none of the equipment ever left inventory.

The equipment supervisor was a Regintian named Bosserbury. Bosserbury was critical and strict with anyone who borrowed equipment.

One day I asked him, "Bosserbury, do you know where this particular apparatus was for the past several days? We've been searching all over for it, and no one knew where it was and suddenly it's here in inventory."

He glared at me as if I were a nuisance. He said, "There must be something wrong with your inventory list, all these tools are closely monitored and all are accounted for."

I was just about to ask him another question when he walked right out of the room. Apparently, he wasn't aware of my position on the management hierarchy. I called his boss using our usual radio wave capabilities, and told him his underling had just rudely left the room. Even though these radio waves were not intended for Bosserbury, everyone within a certain range could 'hear' them.

He re-entered the room irritated. Then, Bosserbury's demeanor suddenly changed as his boss walked in a few minutes later.

Franster, his boss, stared at him and said, "You better co-operative with Farlee. He is here to investigate criminal activity in the station, and he has full authority from the Brotherhood." Bosserbury's demeanor quieted down at this point, which resulted in a more deferential attitude. He was now an alert 'little boy'.

I asked him, "My inventory list is completely up to-date and over a period of time it indicates that this equipment disappears and re-appears without any reason. Why?"

"I honestly do not know what you're talking about. I have no record of unusual disappearances of any equipment."

This game of cat and mouse lasted about fifteen minutes or so with Franster sitting there doing nothing. So I ended the meeting and left. Later on, after reviewing a complete recording of the meeting with our investigation team, everyone felt Franster was in on it.

"We would have expected him to at least back up my interrogation and encourage Bosserbury to remember things or give better explanations, but he sat there and said nothing," I said to the team. "How does everyone feel about secretly monitoring both Franster and Bosserbury?"

Monitoring means allowing secret nanobots to penetrate their bodies and watch what they say and do anytime we desired. Even though equipment existed to read their minds, we didn't have the legal right to do this yet. These two people thought they had the proper counter technology to thwart these spy devices, but the bots I was referring to are super secret, and it wasn't possible to evade them.

The administrator stated, "In addition to continuing this investigation, we'll monitor these two people and a few others for anything suspicious."

The meeting ended, and all we had to do was wait. For the next little while, nothing happened. None of the exploratory equipment disappeared, nothing untoward was said, and the investigation didn't appear to be making any headway.

There was one little hint though. The forensics done on certain pieces of equipment indicated some of it had been to Antarctica, but any records of trips there ended in 1920. Yet Antarctic molecular material on this equipment indicated recent visits within even the last week, but records indicated no visits there at all. Something fishy was going on.

I spoke to Franster about it, "Why are these particular tools covered with molecules from the Antarctic when according to your records there have been no visits there for about 80 years?"

"Farlee, why don't we go to the top balcony of the Station and have a refreshment, I'll be much more relaxed and can bring you up-to-date, OK?"

For a moment, I thought about what the risk would be following him up there considering we were slightly suspicious of him to begin with. "Fine with me," I responded.

Five minutes later, as I entered the recreation room forming the main part of the balcony, I was surprised how empty the place was except for Franster and a person named Masser, the manager in charge of all transportation to the Solar System and Earth areas.

"Hi Farlee, I was just about to leave; have a nice time while you're up here," then he left.

I didn't know what to make of this. This place usually had people hanging around but not this time. There was an undercurrent of suspicion lingering in my mind as I thought about whether this sequence of events was planned or not. Franster pointed to a location near a window with a view of Earth indicating that is where we would have our little meeting. He went to get the refreshments.

As I glanced out the window, I felt tired: a very unusual thing for a Regintian. At this point in my story, Appleton will take over as he has a more detailed perspective as to what happened.

This is Appleton again.

Continuing with Farlee's story, just at the point where the above story left off, there was an attempt on his life. He was incapacitated for a day or two. What the alleged murderers didn't realize was that Farlee was in a cloned Regintian body. This sort of thing is rarely done and is usually used when the life of a Regintian might be at risk. Using a Regintian cloned body reduced the chance of his life being underhandedly terminated.

When an attempt is made to kill a Regintian in that situation, there is a greater chance a person will survive traumatic situations in a cloned body rather than in a normal one. I have to admit, when Farlee made the decision to use a cloned body we all thought he was becoming a bit paranoid since we felt the chances of anything happening to him where incredibly slim. Our people number about a trillion in many thousands of star systems, and murder rarely happens. It's about two or three per Earth year for the entire race of Regintians.

But there you go, Farlee was right; if he hadn't had this cloned body, he definitely would have been killed.

Let me summarize the investigation. The reason Masser, the transportation manager, was in the recreation space to begin with was to ensure there was no one there when Farlee and Franster arrived. He had the power to clear the area. Once Farlee appeared, it was rather easy to deploy poisonous gas to kill him. They of course did not know of Farlee's cloned body, which is far more difficult to destroy with this type of weapon. The plan that Franster and Masser had was to deny they knew anything about Farlee's death or his whereabouts. That would have worked if Farlee had really died, but once he was revived (Franster and Farlee didn't know that was happening) he told the authorities what the sequence of events was, and that was the end of Masser and Franster's career as well as Bosserbury.

Other than those three people, we found three other criminals working for them that were listed as explorers but had somehow escaped the bureaucratic vetting and were abducting humans with certain physical characteristics, extracting sperm and egg cells to make their offspring 'marketable'.

Eventually, we found a lab outside the official expedition bases being managed by what humans would refer to as a criminal syndicate composed of those six people. It was located in the Antarctic. What infuriated us was the transportation manager Masser. He was third in command of the entire Earth expedition and managing the whole black market operation. He was from a very wealthy family and was always searching for profitable opportunities. Somehow, he had managed to fool the Brotherhood into believing he was a solid member of the expedition team. Franster and Bosserbury were part of the syndicate and attempted to kill Farlee with Masser's approval.

The expedition authorities arrested them all, and they are on their way back to Reginta. We completely documented their ill doings and noted they had been abducting humans to extract cell material for years. Whom they abducted depended on the market for specific looking humans. After these black market operators removed the egg and sperm cells, they placed the human 'donators' back where they found or abducted them.

This abduction process was more difficult than it seemed. When the criminals captured and returned them, they had to make sure no one noticed. In addition, they had to prevent our top management personnel from knowing what was going on.

That was the reason for making the humans unconscious when they were abducted. The abductors would then put them back and wake them up, so they would not be aware of what happened and the whole operation wouldn't look suspicious.

Disappearing humans will be missed, disappearing sperm and egg cells will not.

I am going to interrupt my story because one of the members of the Brotherhood Council would like to speak to you directly. He is a sacred member who is involved with galactic ethics and is closely associated with the Spirit Congregation -- who were quite aware of these abductions by the way.

His name is Lovelylosa, and here he is.

Greetings Earthling, I would like to welcome you to Reginta.

I understand that you are one of the many humans who cannot communicate with me, but I do understand that you are quite conscious of our communications to you via your avatar. Let me proceed to what I am about to say.

I would like to sincerely apologize for what has happened. We Regintians have a strong sense of moral ethics and are appalled at what has been going on.

I would also like to mention that this situation is now under complete control, and there will be no more abductions. I guarantee you that.

I also want to apologize for believing that human imagination had conjured up all these alien abduction stories over the years. Unfortunately, we ignored these stories in the past because we thought humans were just imagining them. Now the truth is know and rest assured that if we hear any more stories about humans being abducted, a full investigation on our side will be launched.

Thank you so much for your attention in this matter.

I will now turn you back to Appleton.

Thank you Lovelylosa.

I think this is all we have to say about the Barny and Betty Hill incident.

I have four more stories to fascinate you with. Hescute will handle the two short ones, Eubas is back again with the third one and Erborite for the long one at the end. I think you might have already heard about these through your so-called 'popular' press. The first one is something called the Phoenix lights, the second is Bigfoot/Sasquatch, then the Face on Mars, and finally Heaven's Gate.

OK Hescute, the human has your full attention.

PHOENIX LIGHTS

This might have been one of the most controversial UFO sightings in U.S. history. Even important leaders like the governor of Arizona, claimed they saw it (at least claimed when he retired). We found this incident to be another opportunity to learn more about human behavior. Sometimes irrational human conduct can be overwhelming. I can understand why humans believe in God without seeing physical evidence since we Regintians also follow these beliefs but believing in certain unusual phenomenon based on flimsy evidence? This article will set the record straight on the Phoenix Light controversy.

First, let's lay down some basic facts. U.S. army warthog airplanes occasionally drop flares when being exercised. Even though UFO skeptics have attributed the March 17, 1997 sighting to this, it is not the cause of the Phoenix light incident.

The real cause was by a gentleman (we will not disclose his name) who connected flares to a series of helium-filled balloons and let them loose in the sky about a minute apart. This information was eventually released to the general public about ten years later. So what was the purpose of this? Was it just a hoax or was he doing it for the U.S. military?

The real reason he did it was that *we* wanted him to do it. We knew that these floating lights would cause the general public and the press to speculate quite a bit. This conjecturing is quite normal and happens all the time when people witness unexpected 'in-the-sky' events and other weird things. But quite frankly, we weren't prepared for the paranoia that followed.

The idea for the balloons first came up when we wanted to celebrate a major event in one of our colleague's life. Humans have birthdays, weddings, and many other types of celebrations and anniversaries based on time. Regintians have celebrations as well, but

167

they come about differently. This one is similar to a birthday-awareness celebration with a twist. When you are born into our society, we have a weird (even for us) way of celebrating the event. The beginning of this existence is never mention to the person who is born. During the first few years of his life, this person would have no idea about how his birth or life began. Eventually, after all the education and integration into normal society, he begins to ask questions as to when this happened. That's what we call 'Awareday', and it's when the celebration begins.

A Monitoring Station is located in Arizona of where the exact location is, I am not prepared to say. It just so happens that at this station, we had a very young Regintian who finally figured out he *was* born and on what day. This is always a festive time for us as well as fun for the relationships between the 'Awareday' boy and his colleagues. He was asked how to best celebrate this event and since coincidently he had been watching balloons carrying humans up for pleasure, desired the same thing for himself. We thought it was a good idea but convinced him to launch a much lower level of balloon, and what he chose was a very basic method.

The young Regintian had made an acquaintance with a human located in Arizona. He asked this person to organize this balloon launching as a favor. The person didn't know we were aliens and wasn't aware of our human cloned bodies.

So the balloons went up on that special day. This little event then began to produce headlines all over the world in a way that totally astonished us. We did expect a bit of speculation, maybe even in the press, but not this much.

This pretty well sums up the whole event and now we will proceed to Bigfoot/Sasquatch.

BIGFOOT / SASQUATCH WAS ONE OF US

From time to time, we try to improve our cloning technology. A special portable chamber was modified to decrease the time it took to convert from Regintian to human physiology and had to be tested on Earth. For example, if we were away from our Station Base and someone wanted to appear human or get back to being Regintian in a short period of time, then that person's body would be placed into this portable chamber and his brain transferred to the other body. If we could do this, it would enhance our 'on Earth' productivity because of its portability, so anyone could change their appearance almost at will. It worked quite well on the Lunar-Base and the next step was to try it on Earth.

As a way of testing this chamber in a practical application in the wilderness, a specific day was chosen to allow one of our explorers, along with a colleague, to operate it on a long hike. When the hike was over, he would be in the correct human body form as he arrived at his destination.

Unfortunately, something happened to the human clone, and he ended up resembling a strange beast. Concerned with this unusual effect, they both sought to return to the local Station immediately. Unfortunately, while they were doing that, they bumped into a family get-together fishing on the edge of a river. They started sneaking around them to make sure that those people wouldn't notice the 'strange beast' in his malfunctioning human clone. It almost worked except for the fact that a little girl from that family was scampering around and stumbled on to them.

She screamed, and they both ran but not before one of the human adults saw them. Then the rest of that family rushed up to the little girl and managed to glimpse them as they ran away.

That explorer's creepy look was a result of miscalculating the ability of quickly changing to human form while in that portable chamber. Something happened to the human outward appearance in there as the brain was attaching itself to it. There must have been an unusual bacterium, or something our engineers weren't familiar with, that caused it to evolve.

It just so happens that unusual looking creatures were part of the local legends of that area. This is probably what scared these people into calling the police and next thing you know, there was a helicopter up in the air searching for those two explorers. Later on, they found out that one of them was a police officer taking the day off with his family. That was bad luck for those two explorers.

They spotted a cave and headed straight for it. At the same time, one of the explorers attempted to signal the local Station through his natural radio wave capability but never heard back since the cave environment effectively shielded the radio signals. They stayed in it for a couple of days and finally emerged. There was a possibility the police might still be searching for them.

Finally, one of them received a signal from the Station, and he was told they would be picked up in the morning. Next day, they sent a small spacecraft down to retrieve them and as they began to vacate the cave, they spotted a couple of humans doing something. They hid themselves and watched. One of them had a movie camera, and the other was putting on a gorilla suit. This really peaked their curiosity, so they continued to watch. Once that person had the gorilla suit on, he began to walk away from the person holding the camera.

At first, they thought they were witnessing the filming of a movie, but usually there is a large staff of people on a movie set. Obviously, this was a couple of amateurs having fun. They decided to record it themselves and add it to their usual 'human peculiarities' item list. Watching these people was amusing, so they waved the spacecraft away, and continued to record and monitor their conversations. The eavesdropping they heard amounted to tales of legendary creatures that are alleged to inhabitant the local area.

When the two humans finished their filming, they loaded their equipment in the back of a pickup truck and as they pulled away, the camera they had used fell out of it. At this point, feeling a bit sorry for them -- considering the effort they put into their project -- the explorers retrieved it hoping to return it to them without being noticed.

One of them had an idea; he signaled the spacecraft to pick them up, and then requested the pilot follow the two humans in stealth mode. As they did this, one of the technicians on board examined the reel of film with special sensors that could read through the tape case without destroying the film inside of it. His special sensor revealed that the film was useless because the case had broken when it fell out of the truck and had allowed light to seep in and destroy all of the exposed film. This was the sixties, and it was all chemical based filming for amateurs in those days.

They felt sorry for the two, so they went back to the location where they had originally recorded their film and re-filmed the whole operation by super-imposing the correct chemicals on the exposed film. Since they did not have a gorilla costume, they replaced that figure and filmed it with their own weird looking 'strange beast'. They felt they were not interfering with humans (at least not in a big way) since their own defective clone slightly resembled that person in the gorilla suit to begin with.

This new film was completed in a few minutes with the help of swarming nanobots configured in camera mode. They hurried back to the human's truck and waited for them to come to a complete stop. The spacecraft pilot sent another swarm of nanobots to dispense a special sleeping gas that put them out, while our explorer placed the camera back into it. He then sent in another swarm of nanobots to wake them up, and the humans continued driving without suspecting a thing.

Later on, the humans released the film to the public, and it was purported to be the legendary beast Bigfoot. What an interesting thing to do we thought. These people were actually promoting their little act in the woods as an authentic piece of historical documentation. We felt a bit outlandish having our explorers partake in a deception.

Should we describe this as a dual deception? Our explorer and his colleague deceived two humans, and then those two humans deceived the general public -- or tried to. We consider this little trick to be tolerable; if that camera hadn't fallen out of the truck this event would have happened anyway.

So those two explorers had a firsthand experience with humans in covertly creating a legend or in this case perpetuating it. Imagine that, the famous Bigfoot film, with a truly fictitious creature played by a man in an ape suit, was actually shot by aliens from the planet Reginta.

That was Hescute, thanks Hescute.

FACE ON MARS

We weren't going to bother mentioning the face on Mars, but my young nephew Eubas insisted on it. It was an 'Awareday' present given to his brother back in 1950 by a family member before Eubas was even born. His brother cannot be here since he is on his way back home by cruiser from Earth and should be here in another 150 years. Unfortunately, there are no avatars on that cruiser, and Eubas is therefore filling in for him. I made it conditional that he doesn't use his eyelids again to try to communicate with you. Just the proper translation device please Eubas.

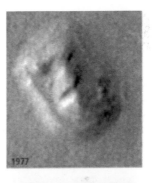

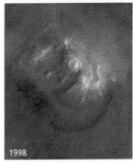

Hello Earthling, I'll be quick with this one. The original face of Mars was an artistic rendering of a human face by my brother to celebrate his 'Awareday' in 1950. It took him a couple of weeks with a standard space shuttle equipped with all sorts of Laser tools and

explosives. At the time he did this, it was considered a lot of fun, and no one thought about the probability of it being discovered by human space probes later on.

When the Viking Orbiter 1 discovered it in 1977, we had to go back to the monument and disrupt it so it wouldn't resemble anything human. The next time a picture was taken of it in 1998, it looks like a pile of rubble. I guess we must have done a good job. Uncle Appleton informs me that it might be restored after we reveal ourselves. If this happens, my brother will be pleased.

I wouldn't bet on it Eubas. OK Erborite, it's your turn again.

HEAVEN'S GATE

The next story I have been allowed to report is a bit sad. I could never get over the devastating events of the Heaven's Gate chronicle. Such a tragic event should never have happened. The person behind this organization believed that aliens from outer space did exist and that was long before we made contact with him. He also believed the spiritual world connected the UFO phenomenon with the real world he was living in.

Marshall Applewhite was his name (also known as Bo or Do), and his initial beliefs, as far as we know, were not based on any encounters with us. At the beginning, his own ideology inspired the contentions regarding his view of the universe. This was to change later on when someone from our expedition team came into contact with him.

This cult fascinated me to the point where I convinced one of our new members, named Sinusblack, into joining the cult around 1995. After reviewing a 1982 film called 'The Mysterious Two', Sinusblack was hooked. We both persuaded the exploration authorities to allow Sinusblack to reveal himself as a Regintian to this group. If they were considered a bunch of UFO weirdoes to begin with and began to advertise the fact that they were communicating with us, it wouldn't make much difference since no one in the conventional news world would believe them anyway. So we figured it wouldn't do any harm to make contact with them.

Sinusblack kept a diary and here is his story about Heaven's Gate and Marshall Applewhite.

I first heard of Heaven's Gate in 1995. My fascination with Marshall Applewhite stemmed from my own attitude about religion. I come from a deeply religious background based on a planet in the same globular cluster as the Regintian sun. It is a spiritual haven for believers and has become a Mecca ever since the existence of God has been scientifically proven. I would venture to say that at least 95% of our population fervently worships God as opposed to only half on Reginta.

When I first landed on Earth, I was as green as they come and had just celebrated my 'Awareday' with our usual customs. Traveling to Earth has been my life's goal. I studied for a long time back on Reginta to become an Earth explorer, and here I am ready for the greatest adventure in my life. Exploring Earth physically is everything I expected and more. I love being in the presence of humans and getting to know them. This fascination is what drove me to learn more about Marshall.

When I first landed on the Lunar-Base, the exploration management did not give me an assignment, so I ended up on one of our Station Bases on Earth in the state of New Mexico and directed to mix with Earthlings to get to know them better. That was in the early part of 1995.

One of the fascinations I had was with Earth belief systems, which not only included their main religions but also cults and pseudoscience, like palm reading, astrology, and extraterrestrials. The extraterrestrial is the most fascinating since I supposedly am one of them. Human perceptions and interpretations about these things have been wild and nonsensical; I desired to know more about why humans can sometimes think so illogically (not that we're perfect of course).

This fascination ultimately led me to the Heaven's Gate cult or movement, as they would call it. I stumbled onto this cult when Erborite showed me a short film called The Mysterious Two and then later viewing a full-page ad in the newspaper USA Today. Within a week, I had joined the group and upon meeting Marshall for the first time, I found him aloof and commanding.

He was a bossy person who wanted to be obeyed. He treated everyone as his subordinate. How did I convince Marshall Applewhite I was a genuine extraterrestrial?

The best way would be to show him my Regintian body, but I wasn't able to get a private meeting with him because of his aloofness.

So I wrote him a letter and explained to him that I was in tune with his beliefs, and I would contact him through his mind at noon the next day. What I did was to send a swarm of nanobots into Marshall's ears that would assemble themselves into tiny loudspeakers and would allow him to think he was receiving my thoughts.

After that was done, he was totally awed. We had a private meeting, and I explained to him that I originated from the planet Reginta and this had to be kept a secret. Later, I would demonstrate my alien body when he visited my living quarters. This would include transferring my brain into my Regintian body.

He came over, witnessed all this, and was stunned. After this experience, he stopped mentioning anything about himself being a walk-in -- a spirit who is using a human body as a container.

There was also a change in his demeanor. His mannerisms and the gaze on his face began to have a detached look. His eyes seemed to open more, which is how our eyes appear to humans who saw them. I always wondered if Marshall was subconsciously making himself appear like us.

In addition, something else set my mind wondering. Did he have one of those guardian angels from the Spirit Congregation imbedded in his mind? Was this possible incident the reason for him formerly insisting he was one of those walk-ins? Otherwise, he was thrilled at meeting me every day and would ask countless questions about our home planet.

One thing I insisted on was that he never mentioned to anyone that I was an 'alien' from a different planet. The punishment was simple; I would immediately disassociate myself from his life. He was so awed by my presence and disclosure, he kept his promise to the bitter end.

One day I had to go back to the Lunar-Base and was startled by a message for me. The expedition manager approached me and explained this message was from some unnamed entity in the Spirit Congregation. I was jaw struck: a young novice like myself getting a communication from a member of the Spirit Congregation! Awesome. Wait until my family back home hears about this.

I nervously took the message in my hand with the manager standing right by me curious to find out what it was. After pressing the button with one of my thumbs . . . nothing happened. The manager had an understanding look on his face and said, "Oh it's one of those. It is meant for you only, and I have to go away."

With that said, the manager walked away, and I took the message container to my room seeking privacy. Once there, I didn't waste any time and pressed the button to activate the message. A 3D holographic image of a Regintian form appeared, and I waited for it to say something.

(Appleton again. To understand what the entity said, I am going to use common Earth linguistics rather than Sinusblack's diary entries so you will have an idea of the significance of the wording.)

"Thou art on holy ground. Bow before for me and enjoy the happiness of our meeting. Thou servith the Lord with sincerity over the years Sinusblack. Thou shalt be rewarded significantly, as thou approachith the end. The Lord requirith your undivided attention to his demands and concerns."

I have never been so nervous in my whole life. To imagine a young and lowly person like myself is now getting attention from the Spirit Congregation. They are actually asking me to help them out. What an incredible privilege this is: to be a servant of the Lord. From what I could tell, the entity was probably a high-level angel even though he didn't really identify himself.

"Young Sinusblack, thou shalt follow these instructions to the last. Thou shalt meet with Marshall Applewhite and bring him peace and solace. This shalt guide him to be ready for the everlasting fulfillment of life, and join with him to achieve these truths."

Suddenly the image stopped. I sat there waiting for something else to happen. It didn't seem normal for this message to have finished so abruptly. But nothing happened, even after waiting an hour.

Never mind; my destiny was to comply with this entity's wishes. Not to waste any more time, I decided to get back to Earth as quickly as possible to be with Marshall and support him in any way I could.

Did Marshall have direct contact with the spirit congregation? The spirit I received the message from was evasive and not very clear. It was a confusing state, but my destiny was to serve and help Marshall in any way I could.

When I got back, Marshall and I continued to spend a lot of time together, and I explained to him that Regintians lived an extremely long life, forever in a practical sense but not in a spiritual sense. We could still die by being killed or murdered. Overall, Marshall was a happy man and asked me if he could remove his body and have his brain placed in a Regintian clone. We have put Regintian brains in humans but never the other way around.

I told him it's never been done before, and I am pretty sure the exploration management would have none of it. He was so adamant about this, he put me under a lot of pressure. After all, the spirits had told me to do anything he desired, so I relented and came up with a plan.

Occasionally Regintians use Regintian clones as a safety precaution for dangerous environments. My plan was to steal one from our next transport visit from Reginta to Earth. Virtually all starships carry a half dozen Regintian clone bodies to be used for emergencies.

They are rarely used. My plan was to steal one, since they probably wouldn't notice its absence for a long time, bring it down to Marshall's residence and place his brain in it.

As I mentioned before, the main problem is that a human brain has never been transformed successfully into these clones, and it was unknown if it would work. I explained this to Marshall, but he was still adamant about switching his body.

Behind the scenes, Marshall was plotting. He had convinced members of his cult that there was a spaceship coming right behind the Hale-Bop comet, and they should commit suicide to ensure their journey on that spaceship. I didn't know any of that.

Immediately after the majority of the members committed suicide, Marshall came over to my place, and we performed the transfer. Something went wrong. I could see Marshall wasn't responding, and he stayed unconscious. I panicked and called my administrator on the Lunar-Base and explained the situation to him. As expected, I was severely reprimanded.

With the support of a colleague, I transferred Marshall's empty body and his new Regintian body to one of our Monitoring Stations. They couldn't help him, so we placed his Regintian body on one of our shuttles with the intent of transferring him up to the Lunar-Base. We transferred his human body back to his home, and that's when I discovered all the suicides. When seeing this, I was dumbstruck and didn't know what to think. I quietly left there and made my way back to our shuttle.

It was too late for Marshall; his brain had deteriorated so much that it was pointless trying to restore it. The only happy campers on this day were the Spirit Congregation. As to whether Marshall is now happy or got his wish, there is only one way to find out. .
.

As I write these last sentences, I feel devastated. Some questions are burning inside of me. Is the Spirit Congregation being fair with both Marshall and me?

Was Marshall's desire to be transferred to a Regintian clone a real desire on his part or a suggestion planted in this mind by a guardian angel? Did Marshall know he was going to die once the transfer happened?

The container holding that last message from the Spirit Congregation was incapable of sending messages the other way. I had no way of really knowing if my prayers were being listened to since I didn't even know if I had my own guardian angel. I need to know; I am desperate to know. There is only one sure way to find out.

I have to visit the spiritual world and that means one thing as far as I am concerned. We all know by now what the rules are; suicide will get me there. Travelling to the other side is the only way of finding out . . . but I'm not all that sure.

What I am about to inform you is not approved by the Regintian Brotherhood nor the Exploration Management of Earth but . . . I do . . be . . ve . . .that it . . . me . . .a. . . .gf.g. . . . d.. . .v.v. . . .nn

Opps . . . One day I'll have to sort out that cut off point in this recording.

Oh it's me, Erborite again.

And that is the last entry I am disclosing from Sinusblack's diary.

It was obvious to me that Marshall had become a direct member of the Spirit Congregation. After observing the lifeless Regintian body on the way to Lunar-Base, Sinusblack committed suicide. This made me feel sad since I had become close to him in the short time I came to know him.

What was all that commotion about the Hale-Bopp comet? Sinusblack told me the comet had no significance other than a ploy to entice the members of his group to commit suicide. Marshall's real ticket to the other side was to become closer to the Spirit Congregation in any way he could and eventually meet his members there. Sinusblack actually became a member of Marshall's troop and started to believe in almost everything Marshall believed in.

As far as the rest of the diary is concerned, we only want you to hear the main part of it. The very last section is classified, but don't worry we will be releasing it sometime in the future. I will confirm however that Sinusblack is in the spirit world right now, but I won't state whether he or Marshall is in heaven or purgatory.

You will find out after we reveal ourselves. Right now, there is no point in doing that. As per the Treaty of Spiritual Truth, we are not allowed to disclose this information.

PART 4: OFFICIAL COMMUNICATION

REVEALING OURSELVES

This is Appleton again.

Our current policy of officially revealing ourselves has to be prepared cautiously and methodically. One of the problems I know we'll encounter is the likelihood that people might associate us with all the wacko-pseudoscientific allegations of UFO visits that have happened regularly all over the world. As we have been explaining in this book, the vast majority of these allegations are strictly illusions and fabrications. So let me take this opportunity to enlighten your human minds and dismiss all those rumors that have been attributed to non-existent UFO and extraterrestrial visits (us that is).

If this book was some kind of science fiction novel, then the next paragraph might be considered a spoiler. Realize that I'm not in the business of spinning fantasy yarns for the purposes of entertainment.

The following is a short list of people who have been made fun of or suspected to be possible aliens from outer space. These people are famous, and if this were a proper fiction novel, I would wait until a certain amount of storyline had accumulated and then exposed the truth in the most entertaining of ways with plot climaxes and storybook endings etc.

Without further ado, let's begin this account of celebrated persona.

We did not ever abduct or replace any of the following people:

Prime Minister Silvio Berlusconi of Italy: check with his female friends and they will inform you he still behaves with his own 'normality'.

Donald Trump: he was not one of us either, but I must admit that he had me fooled at one point, as there was a person back home that wanted to visit Earth but didn't have permission. He was in the clothing business, and we thought he had sneaked on to Earth and became 'the Donald'. But after a full investigation, we realized Donald

Trump was a real human. His birth certificate was real as well.

Vladimir Putin of Russia: if he was one of us, he would have left the 'Pussy Riot' group alone.

Nancy Pelosi: we have never supplied any cloning technology to her.

Monica Lewinsky: we tried to get into politics during Carter's time and Obama's time, not Bill Clinton's time.

Bill Maher: If we ever run again as Democrats, we'll get in contact with him.

Hugo Chávez: Some of our people have mentioned that he does resemble us a little bit; it's strictly a coincidence.

Arnold Schwarzenegger: He is definitely not one of us; just ask his domestic help.

Joe Biden: I was about ready to admit he was one of our agents, but I checked our records twice before I discovered he wasn't. There is no way Regintians are that 'funny'.

Paul Ryan: not one of us, if he was, he would have helped to increase spending to get ready for our revelation.

Ross Perot: we don't like him. He was ready to expose us before we were ready.

Dennis Kucinich: he confuses us, we thought only right-wingers believed in UFOs . . . but then there is Jimmy Carter!

Paul Hellyer: Former Canadian defense minister and UFO believer . . . I don't know why I'm mentioning this person . . . maybe Canadians will be more helpful to us when we reveal ourselves.

George Lucas: not one of us, at least not from this galaxy.

Steven Spielberg: Could never be one of us. He doesn't even know what an alien looks like.

Bill Gates: Definitely not one of us. The BSOD (Blue Screen Of Death) disappeared in Vista and Windows 7. If he was one of us, he would have kept it.

Internet Clouds: The Spirit Congregation originally designed this as a way of integrating with the new world techno era, however, Google, Apple, and Microsoft stole the idea. Someone from one of those companies must have had a direct link to the Spirit Congregation and secretly stole the idea without the Congregation's approval; serves the Congregation right in my view.

As of the beginning of November 2012 we do not have any clones representing abducted humans anywhere in the world, so that leaves out Rick Perry x Ron Paul (RP^2) as UFO abductees.

Let me continue with building the case for the Earthling / Regintian summit.

Not only was the 20th and early 21st centuries the most remarkable time in human history, it was also a moment of realization for us. There was nothing in our history that could compare with it. We are certainly more advanced scientifically, technologically, and spiritually (a very different view of spirituality no doubt), but we acquired this knowledge in a linear time frame over a much longer period of time. Humans ventured forth to the moon approximately eight to ten thousand years from the beginning of their agricultural revolution, while we took about 350,000 years. As of this day, most of the scientific knowledge humans have acquired has risen in an exponential surge in the last two centuries. This astonishing progress initialized our thinking as to whether we should consider making official contact with humans either directly or through their governments.

There was one little problem: Democracy!

We knew about the experimentation with it in ancient Greece, and then nothing for centuries. Then a bit of tinkering with it in the British Empire, as it began to evolve when its House of Commons, and related institutions, slowly emerged. The newly formed United States of America solidified the concept even more.

To be quite honest with you, we felt it wouldn't last; it just wasn't suitable for intelligent people like humans and us. Well wouldn't you know it, since the 19th and 20th centuries were a time of change and even revolution, it almost guaranteed that this remarkable political philosophy would catch on. Like everything else in the 20th century, this governing system spread so fast it caused nothing but confusion for us. Our attitude towards your advancement was in fact the slowest thing to change. The majority of states on Earth now have democracy.

It wasn't until about 1950 when we realized it was here to stay, and we'd better get use to it. Even though we have superior scientific knowledge and technology and are actually more intelligent than you humans are, there is still trouble comprehending the various subtleties of your political systems. Just as we begin to understand the ideology behind certain political institutions and parties, we blunder. And what makes it even more confusing is that millions of humans make these same mistakes.

We noticed an increase in social conflict within most western democracies starting with what Americans called the Vietnam War. At the same time, a new music movement began in the UK with groups of musicians like the Beatles. We also notice they had longer than normal hair for the times along with different social behavior and were influential with younger people. These new changes exposed our ineptness in responding quickly to the shifting times, especially concerning the social order.

Here's an example of what I mean. To unravel our confusion about democracy, our management allocated a large group of 'explorers' to spend time in various important countries during the late sixties. They were told to blend in to both the top and root levels of your communities. The top part was anyone elected into government office, particular in federal governments, and the root level was to mix with the so-called hippie movement. This would ensure proper assimilation within your societies and try to understand humans in this 20th century by mingling with you.

In the mid 1970s, one of our people had a brilliant idea. If we were to reveal ourselves to humanity, why not do it through this hippie culture. We were so use to the relatively slow pace of human development from centuries past that it confused our understanding of rapid cultural changes and thought this hippie association might be an excellent way of doing it. After all, these young people will be tomorrow's leaders and if we became their friends right from the beginning, we would be in a better position to deal with them as they matured and progressed.

Easier said than done; if humans in the 20th century normally confused us, mingling with this 'sub-culture' was confusion on an exponential scale. To appear like we were blending in, we had to consume drugs, attend protest marches, and vote democrat or for left wing candidates (we were able to alter electoral records to deceive voting bureaucrats into believing we were American and other nation's citizens).

Many of our explorers altered the way their cloned bodies appeared -- e.g. longer hair, less clean clothing, and only occasionally take a shower. They studied the hippie movement right from its Germanic roots and beatnik generation from the 1950s. Hippies did not trust established institutions and middle class values, were against the Vietnam War, and sought to ban nuclear weapons. They thought highly of certain characteristics of Hindu culture, were sexually liberated, and leaned towards vegetarian diets. Drugs became a big part of their way of life, and they viewed them as enhancing their consciousness.

The main advantage in associating with this hippie movement was the far more tolerant people linking with us, rather than the usual mainstream. Normally, even with our authentic looking cloned human bodies, we are rather awkward when it comes to integrating with human manners and customs. Not so with these hippies; they considered our behavior to be quite normal.

For example, we have a bad habit of always smiling. We do this because we yearn to be accepted and simply overdo it. With the hippie culture, this idiosyncrasy wasn't an issue, and they never considered us weird or awkward. They just assumed we were on drugs, and that's why we behaved this way.

Throughout this process, we believed our understanding of humans would grow but when the seventies came, the hippie movement began falling out of favor around the world. This caught us off guard since we assumed everything would become hippieish, but it didn't. We were actually taking drugs every day even though it was slowing destroying our cloned bodies. They had to be constantly replaced . . . oh well. . .

But having said this, the fizzling out of the hippie movement didn't deter one of our agents on the inside. That was Josiwe. He was determined to blend in and work his way up through some hierarchy. There was one little problem. I am openly admitting this to you right now, but the confusing and somewhat naïve approach we took trying to integrate with humans was a problem. Although our management had completely embraced the idea of blending in with hippie culture, pre-20th century beliefs influenced most of our social knowledge of humans. The 20th century was different. Many of our staff explorers, who stayed on the exploration team for an average of 450 years, saw the movement towards democracy as temporary. For some strange reason, the hippie culture was seen as more permanent.

They thought this 'vision' of theirs was good enough to comprehend human thinking but in the long run, it didn't work. Yes some 'hippies' did turn out to be leaders and important people but certainly not all of them. As with any group of people with a unique culture, only a few can achieve power or influence; it all depends on chance and knowing the right people. We seemed to be getting nowhere despite Josiwe's convictions. He was always going to mad parties and protest rallies. The people he associated with rarely acquired any substantial power.

There was something else about Josiwe that I didn't particularly admire. At the beginning of his assignment, he was both naïve and rather conceited. The naïve part wasn't too unusual given the circumstances. Most of us are naïve when integrating with human culture for the first time. His arrogant manner was the real problem. As a matter of fact, some of us were so disgusted with his attitude and behavior that I can't begin to describe what his introduction to humanity was like.

One good thing about him was his habit of meticulously detailing his experiences while on Earth through both a diary and a recording. So what I'm about to do is place a few paragraphs from a recording of his done in real time when he was just getting started, and you the reader can decide for yourself whether this drivel is worth reading.

I am so grateful for meeting that stranger a few hours ago who directed me to this enterprise. We had a brief political discussion, and I told him I wasn't highly experience relating to men and women in both a spiritual and physical sense. When he spoke to me, it was obvious he wanted to help me out.

"You just leave it to me man, I'll help you out. I know this incredible place that will give you anything you want," he said as he winked at me. I am not entirely sure what that wink meant. I have been told in my human indoctrination class on Reginta that humans use it when they mean they're OK. I am not even sure what that means.

"Just go downtown to a place called the Whole Earth Meeting Place, and I am definitely sure they will satisfy you."

This is the beginning of my role in integrating myself with human culture, I thought. He sounds genuinely sincere, and I am quite happy having met him. I follow his instructions and go to this place. I am entering the front door to the Whole Earth Meeting Place. I notice this lovely woman sitting at a reception desk smiling at me. Her attitude appears to be the embodiment of the new age spirit in human progressiveness.

I approached her and she says, "Hi, how are you?"

"I am fine thank you," I say in my friendliest tone and facial expression.

"We have many ways of helping and pleasing you, why don't you come into this room, and we can go over what your requirements are," she says in a most pleasing manner.

At this point, I'm imagining how easy it is to blend into and become part of this new human thinking. I suppose humans are finally getting rid of their propensity to wage war, and this openhearted friendliness is a new way of uniting humanity. She is making me feel quite comfortable. I am determined to learn everything I can about the new-age good manners. This will only help to achieve a high level of inter-human relationships. We enter a small room with comfortable armchairs and a sofa.

"Please sit down here," she says as she points to the sofa. She sits across from me in one of the armchairs.

"Is there any refreshment I can get for you?"

"I'll be fine with water." After I say that, she smiles at me with a curious gaze.

As she rises from her armchair, I'm not quite sure about the clothing she is wearing. She appears very naïve and sweet, and I don't have the heart to tell her that the shirt she is wearing tends to reveal a lot of her legs all the way up her body. Conversely, I have no experience in dealing with humans of her sex, age, and culture, so I decide to keep my mouth shut.

She leaves the room for a moment and comes back with two drinks. The other one is for her presumably. When she hands me mine, she sits down on the sofa beside me rather than the armchair. The problem with her skirt doesn't go away, and I am starting to feel a bit sorry for her.

"Did Bill tell you the price?" she says.

"Do you mean that person who directed me to your place?" I say.

"Yes, that was probably Bill," she says as she moves closer to me. "It's not very expensive, and you will have a lot of privileges when it's over." She moves again and is now so close her knee is touching mine.

I'm not sure what she's referring to, so I say, "How much is what and what privileges are you talking about?"

"It's $100 up to midnight and $200 overnight, and the privileges are left up to your imagination." She is now grinning from ear to ear, and her eyes take on a slightly different shape. Let me contemplate for a second; I am trying to balance my curiosity at what she is doing and saying without revealing my total ignorance of human social customs.

Suddenly her hand touches my thigh, and then proceeds towards were my two legs meet on my central torso. I believe humans call this the crotch area. I thought for a second that she was attempting to stimulate my 'nonexistent vitals'...

Appleton here.

Sorry for the interruption; I believe we might have mentioned this before, but Regintians do not have genitals on our human cloned bodies. They are of no use to us.

Back to Josiwe.

I purged the idea from my mind of letting her continue. That would be rude on my part, and she did not appear to be a rude person. As I cross my legs to prevent her from accessing my ... uh ... crotch area, I decide to thank her for her 'friendliness'.

So I say, "Excuse me miss ... ah ..."

"Angela," she says with that smile.

"I know you are a friendly person ... and want me to be your friend ... and I want to be your friend ... even a good friend ... eventually ..."

After I mention that, Angela still keeps smiling at me but the look of her eyes changes to a somewhat curious look ... I think. I continue, "Tell me how you can help me, and be specific on the privileges you're referring to." After I mention that, I move my body about a foot away from her on the sofa. That simple little action causes a subtle change in the way she looks at me. Her eyebrows change shape slightly indicating confusion.

"Well . . . what exactly are you here for?" the last two words are slightly higher pitched.

"I want to improve my relationship to people in both a physical and spiritual sense."

"Uh huh . . ." she is now leaning her chin on her fist and has her elbow on her thigh.

"And describe to me what problems you're having with the physical part."

What kind of a question is that, I thought. "Well . . . I don't have physical problems as such; at least a doctor wouldn't call them problems."

"I see," she says. "Don't worry," she takes my hand. "I know exactly what you're talking about, and I can help. I'll even do it for free the first time if you become a regular customer. Let's go into the next room."

She takes my hand firmly and brings me into the next room, which appears to be a luxurious bedroom. Now I know what she is and what she wants to do. I have made up my mind, and I want to get out of here as . . . tactfully as possible.

She walks up to the bed holding my hand and as she sits down on the edge, she attempts to pull me down with her.

I stand my ground and say, "Ah . . . my dear, I don't think you know what I want. I seek both physical and spiritual experiences, but I wouldn't mind delaying the spiritual part until later."

She obviously wants me to pray with her, otherwise what is the purpose of us sitting at the edge of the bed? After that little statement of mine, she releases my hand, places a few of her fingers on her forehead, and has a confused look on her face.

"Spiritual part?" she says. "What spiritual part are you talking about?"

193

"Well I don't want to pray right now; I want you to show me some physical exercise that will allow me to better co-ordinate my body mannerisms."

"I think I know what you mean, but wouldn't you rather do it with a woman?"

What did she mean by that?

Then suddenly, her eyes open up and she says, "Are you gay?"

As far as the Earth/Regintian dictionary was concerned, the word gay means 'to be happy' and even though I don't really feel all that happy at the present time, I try to be polite, so I respond, "Yes."

"Don't worry about a thing. We do that sort of thing as well. Let me get Mike."

She walks out of the room and comes back in a few seconds with a man who has hair down to his shoulders and a gleeful look on his face. At least I think it's gleeful. As she begins to walk out of the room, she takes one last look at me before closing the door and says, "Good luck."

"Hey, how ya doin' man. My name is Mike." He takes my hand and shakes it. "I'm happy to meet you. Did Angela explain everything to you; I mean about the price and times. It's 100 bucks till midnight and 200 bucks overnight." His hand is now on my shoulder kind of pinching it. "Hey man, you gotta lot of muscle there," he's grinning as he says that.

As I examine the facial hair coming off his upper lip, I notice he has a tooth missing.

"What kind of exercise are we going to do?"

Mike chuckles at my statement and answers, "The happy kind." At this point even my inexperience doesn't prevent me from realizing how unprofessional these people are. I invent an excuse to get out of there quickly, and leave.

Overall, I feel this experience has been good for me . . . I think.

Appleton again.

Is there a difference between an escort service and a dating service?

I personally don't know and have never bothered investigating it. You can decide for yourself if this is of any significance.

Continuing with his haughty attitude, here is a little story about him that I was personally involved with. As Josiwe gained experience on Earth, he became completely involved with the hippie counter-culture. Sometimes he was so full of drugs it prevented his biologically based global positioning device (how we keep track of where he is on the planet) from working.

I remember one time I was told to go down and find him but was instructed to go only on a specified date. I arrived around 10 AM in this so-called community center, and my human nose was suddenly filled with terrible smells. I wasn't use to a cloned body, and I couldn't take these smells.

So I went back to my hidden shuttle, got out of the human body, switched to my own body, and went searching for him at night. I thought that what I was doing might be a bit dangerous since these people have never seen an alien before, but I did have a shield cloak on, which made me somewhat invisible. My strategy was to linger in dark areas as much as possible to give me a stealth edge, and then sneak back into that community center and try to find him.

Off I went, and it wasn't too long before I was spotted. There was so much cigarette smoke in that building that it clung to my shield and gave me the appearance of a ghost. The first person who saw me fainted. The next person screamed at the top of her lungs and ran away yelling.

What should I do now? I ran out of the building and out of sheer luck, found a dark lane on the side of it. As I entered this laneway, I tripped on something and fell smack down onto the concrete and asphalt. A human was lying on the ground intoxicated with drugs; I could smell the stench but being in my Regintian body I could also turn the smell off. Unfortunately, when I fell it caused my cloaking mechanism to shut off, and I was completely exposed. Now was the time to get back to the shuttle. At this point, I had to slow down to avoid anyone seeing me. So I crept along the side of the building and bumped into a group of people who started to laugh when they saw me.

One of them said, "Wow that's fantastic," and they continued on their way.

By now, I was totally confused and once the coast was clear, I started running back to the shuttle. Next thing you know I came across yet another group of people, but this time they had a couple of small kids with them: same reaction, just a lot of laughter and no fear. This was strange indeed. When I had the cloaking device on, they screamed and fainted as I had walked through that smoky environment. When it was shut off, they all laughed and admired me. Realize that at this point we had been studying humans for about 50,000 years and thought we understood them fairly well.

When I got back to the shuttle, I contacted someone at headquarters, and they couldn't understand what was going on either. It was suggested to me that since I wasn't scaring anyone right now why don't I go back and try to find Josiwe.

So back I went and met more smiling people who weren't scared. I re-entered that same building, which still had the aura of cigarette smoke and drugs, and started to wander around. The rock music made the place very noisy.

I bumped into someone who was obviously on drugs. He glared at me and said, "Hey man you look out of this world, heh heh heh heh heh . . . what planet do you come from man . . . hey hey hey hey . . . can I come with you . . . please please please . . . oh come on man . . please don't ignore me. I am ready to go and travel with you. And . . . I got a huge stash of 'stuff' ready to take with us . . . know what I mean man." As he said that, he winked at me.

Now I am totally confused. All my training with humans over the years was absolutely no help in this situation. I decided to ignore him since I couldn't speak to him anyway -- not having my translator with me. I rushed by him and strode up to the second floor of the building where Josiwe was last heard from. As I entered the first room, I tripped over something again (I didn't fall down this time). It was yet another human lying down on the floor, completely out of it. I observed the surroundings, and even though there was a group of people there, they ignored me. They didn't bother to look and see who had entered the room. It wasn't too difficult to figure out they were ignoring me because there was a drug session going on at the time.

Next thing you know the person lying down on the floor stood up, gawked at me, and said, "What the fuck." Talk about an 'oops' moment. I wasn't sure what to do here. When that person began communicating with me in our usual manner, I was startled.

He grabbed me, pulled me into another room, and said, "What the hell are you doing here?" It was Josiwe. I told him I was looking for him and that the expedition management wanted him off Earth.

He said, "No way, I'm staying here."

I said rather forcefully, "Listen to me Josiwe, the whole operation isn't getting anywhere since the people you hang out with have no influence or power."

"Appleton, I am staying, and that is that. And by the way, why are you down here without your human body?" I explained to him why I did it and he said, "Lucky for you it's an American celebration called Halloween, and that's why people are laughing at you. That's also why you were told to come down on this specific date just in case something went wrong, you could always use the Halloween excuse to give yourself a disguise edge. They think your alien look is a fantastic costume, and their laughter is actually a compliment. When you walk back to the shuttle, remember to play it cool as if you really are a human with a Halloween disguise."

Sounds like Josiwe could be right on this one. Just as we were leaving the building, something unexpected happened. We bumped into the hippie who longed to come with me, and he had four of his friends with him.

The first thing he said as he looked at his colleagues was, "Seeee. . . I told you so. A real genuine alien from outer space hey hey hey hey . . ."

His friends just stood there completely startled and staring at me not knowing what to do. I looked at Josiwe, and he looked at me.

Josiwe said, "Hey . . . nice meeting you guys, now we gotta go."

"Oh can we just ask you a few questions please please please. . ." That was the only female of the group speaking. "My name is Mary and this is Allen, Fred, Joe, and Eddy you've already met."

"What would you like to ask us?" responded Josiwe.

"Ouu, ah, you know . . . we want to know where you're from, and what you're doing here, and can you help us?" said Eddy.

I asked Josiwe if these guys were high on drugs just now, and he responded, "They could be but even if they weren't, they'd still be bugging us right now I'll guarantee you that."

Now everyone was asking questions while still being deferential. Eddy disappeared for a moment, and when he returned, he had five more people with him.

One of them said, "I bet that guy's a fake. It is Halloween, isn't it? Somebody go up there and poke him to see if that's just a costume he's wearing."

Josiwe was quick to speak up, "Ah, just a minute guys, it's up to you if you want to believe he's a real alien. We really don't care what you think. Just don't be rude, go up, and start poking him and trying to lift things up. I would think that's really bad manners. Like I said, if you don't believe he's an alien, I couldn't care less. OK?"

That little blurb from Josiwe seemed to cool things down a bit until we could figure out how I could leave without a big scene. Mary spoke up and said, "You definitely are a real alien and some of us here are astute enough to know why you've come. We know you're bringing the new world order, and we're so please you're here."

I radioed to Josiwe, "Get me out of here."

He said, "The best thing to do is to play along with them until I can sneak you out when everyone is sleeping or something like that."

But the opposite happen. By morning, the neighborhood just outside the building had about a hundred people camping waiting to meet me. I was getting desperate and didn't fancy doing anything controversial or violent. There were ways of getting me out but they were unorthodox, like putting everyone to sleep with a knockout gas or something similar. The more time went on, the more appealing that option looked.

"I've got an idea", said Josiwe. "If we put them to sleep with some of your special gas, someone will know and write about it in a newspaper or do a video for the TV news. We don't want any publicity so let me do this. I have this fake drug I can hand out that would look like it's getting everyone high, while really putting them to sleep. That way if a news reporter finds out about it, at least some people could claim that it is the 'usual hippie high' that is causing all these sightings of meeting a real live alien."

Josiwe went ahead, handed out the drugs, and told them it was from the alien. He also told them that these were special drugs and would link them to a new world order etc. Neither Josiwe nor I were surprised when they all believed him and just soaked it all up.

Next thing you know, people fell into a normal sleep and at an opportune time, I sneaked out and returned to the shuttle. I had originally parked it in an out-of-the-way place near a lane-way leading into a dump.

I've never felt so elated as when I squatted in that pilot's station to get the hell off this planet, without Josiwe of course. Later, when I got back to the lunar headquarters, we had a meeting to discuss the day's events and what to do about him.

Then I discovered that the hippie who had first confronted me had actually found the shuttle and had stowed away on it, but had become unconscious since the correct Oxygen ratio wasn't what he was used to. Humans are used to about 20 to 25% oxygen content, while we are used to about 10% content. Fortunately, we discovered him soon enough and were able to revived him and place him in a separate room with the correct air mixture for his physiology. Then we put him to sleep and brought him back home the next day.

RUNNING FOR THE DEMOCRATS

Despite Josiwe's unusual independence from the Regintian expedition, it had no effect on the raging debate that was going on: how and when to officially reveal ourselves to humans. The idea of having some of our people penetrate and blend into human society was still a valid one. And since we were constantly following politics, someone came up with the idea that maybe having a few politicians in power might be a way of handling controversies that might come up when we reveal ourselves later on.

Now here is the weird thing about understanding humans especially when it comes to political candidacy. Most of us Regintians consider ourselves superior to humans in intelligence. But there are things that make me doubt this superiority complex of ours and that is trying to understand the hippie movement in the 60s and 70s, and later on the Republican Party nomination process in 2012.

Just when we thought we have mastered the art of politically manipulating certain types of left or right wing aficionados, we state something that sounds like it's the right thing to say and are soundly rejected. A human candidate says something equally ignorant, and he is cheered.

I am going to introduce you to Rukey who will give you a play by play of what happened by way of a recorded video when we chose to run for office. Unfortunately, Rukey is not physically present.

Our strategy was to elect one person to congress, one person to the U.K. parliament, and one person to the Russian parliament. That was it for the time being. If this plan was successful, we would then proceed to elect more members until we had about 100 people spread throughout these countries. This plan would allow us to deal with paranoia in the political-spheres

of these important countries when we are officially introduced to humankind.

We concluded that our association with the hippie movement should stay the same when Jimmy Carter ran for a second term. At this point in time, we were quite positive that this movement was the wave of the future. A big moment came when a candidate was ready to run for a U.S. congressional district, which was near the location our shuttlecraft was normally stationed. This location will remain a secret but who knows, it might be revealed sometime in the future.

Our candidate did acquire the nomination to represent the Democratic Party, but it was won under very unusual circumstances of which we're still not fully aware of what happened.

The candidate we chose was Josiwe: yes, that same arrogant individual who was highly connected with the Brotherhood back on Reginta. Our expedition forces were cursed with these unprofessional influences from back home, where the only qualification was whose family member they were related to in the Brotherhood hierarchy.

As Josiwe's human experiences grew, he had fallen in so much with the hippie culture that he constantly dressed and behaved like them. When he registered to run for the party nomination in this same district, hardly anyone noticed him despite his weird appearance. To demonstrate how integrated he had become, here are some of his opinions when speaking to him in English.

> Hey man, Give peace a chance.
> Make love, not war.
> Hell no, we won't go.
> Power to the People.
> Drop acid not bombs.
> Live and let live.
> Sock it to me.
> Outtasight!

Right on.
Groovy.
Go with the flow.
Far out, man.
Jump the lines, man!
F*ck the establishment.

As you can see, speaking to Josiwe was rather a frustrating experience. All of these plagiarized phrases were from existing hippie-speak. As time went on, he was never invited to the democratic candidacy debates.

"They're afraid of me, man. They're scared I might make them look like fools."

Josiwe had absolutely no experience debating any human whatsoever, but his confidence was overwhelming even though he rarely made speeches.

"Don't worry about speeches; those things won't help. It's a reform minded mind that will help not traditional election methods."

He received no advice from politically savvy humans and made all decisions himself with a little support from a few inexperience human friends. Important publicity or recognition weren't available from anyone or anything. The whole project was heading for a complete disaster except for one little thing.

At the time, there was an intense rivalry between two other newcomers for this candidacy in addition to Josiwe. The district was democratic, the current congressional representative had retired, and these two people, who had worked for the party in that district for a long time, hated each other. This resulted in a slugfest. What could this internal party squabbling do to Josiwe's chances of winning?

As these two people were viciously attacking each other, district members of the party were fed up. When it came time to vote, those party members were so turned off they voted for Josiwe out of frustration, since they still wanted to vote.

Next thing you know, He won by one vote! I was stunned.

Later, when the real election for congress began and dealing with political nuances became crucial, he demonstrated how ineffective he was when he did not receive any publicity whatsoever for the election campaign, other than the usual party backed stuff.

Some of the things he would do were: stand on a street corner handing out flowers to passersby; the things he didn't do were: interviews with local radio and TV stations. He didn't feel he was verbally gifted enough to handle that type of conversation. This is a problem all Regintians appear to have even with our perfect translator skills down to the correct accent. So guess what?

He lost. We were truly disappointed. Could it have something to do with the hippie clothing and long hair down to his shoulder blades, or the fact that he was occasionally seen smoking pot. And those shoes he wore, or I should say didn't wear; the public always saw him barefoot. He had a 'yuck' factor and whoever did notice him was usually turned off.

It just so happened, that Josiwe's hippie look was on the wane. This is a problem Regintians had in the 20th century. We had no trouble keeping up with scientific and technological advancements but sociological was different. It was a problem for us: not that we lacked the technology or intelligence, but our own culture misinterpreted everything about human behavior.

In our Regintian societies, fast moving social experiences don't exist and during the 50,000 years that our knowledge of humans grew, their progress was usually done at a reasonable pace -- until the 20th century.

Eventually, we dropped the whole idea of connecting with a hippie culture. Later, Ronald Reagan became president and the hippie movement fizzled.

So did our understanding of humans.

THIS TIME RUNNING FOR THE REPUBLICANS

Appleton again.

I hope we're not tiring you out with all this talk about politics, because there's more to come. After that bad experience, we decided to wait a while before entering the political fray again. On returning to this fray many years later, we went with the so-called 'right' this time. Judging by the way they looked and carried out their daily lives, they appeared to be more acceptable to the mainstream public. As time went on, our politically astute explorers developed a heavy bias towards the 'radical right', which I believe is also called the social or religious right. From what we could tell, they had a lot of influence within the Republican Party, and if they saw one of our people constantly preaching their ideology then we stood a good chance of getting elected . . . we hoped . . .

Rukey is going to take over again with another video.

We removed Josiwe from Earth, and he is now on his way back to Reginta. I am the new person in charge of political penetration for Earth. There will be no more interference from well-connected, high handed, conceited relatives situated high up in the Brotherhood hierarchy. I can assure you that.

As for myself, I have no connections to those people other than being chosen by them because of my rather extensive experience in dealing with political situations . . . at least political situations on Reginta.

I carefully studied the political state of affairs during the George W. Bush administration, and I thought this conservative era would continue right after him. There was something that caught our eye during the 2008 political campaign and that was the appointment of Sarah Palin as the vice-presidential nominee. At that particular time, I was looking for a model to emulate and follow, to make sure we didn't do

what we did last time during the 1970s. I wanted to avoid the mistakes of that last experience with the hippies: getting into to a left-wing philosophy that we thought had popular support but was on the wane. Even though McCain and Palin lost the election, I assumed the Palin legacy would be around for a long time to come.

The Palin mentality appeared to be on the rise from 2008 to 2012, so I thought our best chance was to mimic her style and philosophy. Then as the likelihood of her running for the Republican Party nomination went down, we seriously considered seeking the nomination of that party for president of the United States. If we had this candidacy and won the election, it would put us in an incredible position to control almost everything when finally revealing our presence on Earth.

Another key indicator that we were on the right course was the rise of the Coffee Party. This new organization maintained the Sarah Palin momentum that was built up in the 2008 campaign.

This is Appleton again. Excuse me for interrupting this video:

Unfortunately, most of us Regintians are not familiar with human food since we don't eat it.

Yes, our human cloned bodies do appear to consume food from time to time, but this is merely for appearance sake, and the mashed up food is discarded at the end of the day and is definitely not digested.

So why would he call the Tea Party the Coffee Party? Just another Regintian who is not up to date on human beverages, that's all.

One other thing before we continue this video. This little mistake was supposed to have been corrected, but Rukey went on holidays the day this book was published. It was considered such a small mistake we didn't bother dubbing it with a correction.

One more thing before we continue this video: Rukey will be back in about 227 years.

OK, back to the video.

So we chose a cloned Regintian who was the most infiltrated person we've ever had. He had been working his way through the Republican Party for years and became an enormous fan of Sarah Palin. He was not as arrogant as Josiwe, was a bit of a bumbler, but he did come from an influential family back home that was well connected. Who was this influential family? . . . My family!

He is my son, and for now let's name him Bari Tone while not exposing his Earth name (I wish to protect him). This experience he had should make him a strong contender, and American Republicans should take him seriously. This knowledge will also guarantee his elevation to a junior member of the Regintian Brotherhood.

One thing I would like to state here is that I will not be informing you which candidate Bari was cloned into as a person for the 2012 nomination. Nor will I state what that person was supposed to have done for a living before he/she sought the nomination: whether he/she was a public figure, businessperson, male/female or elected politician. The only thing I will state is that he/she ran for the nomination in a human cloned body (obviously). I will also be using the 'he/her' pronouns for convenience without admitting the sex.

I am doing this to guard the secret of who the nominee was as a human candidate. The reason for this is simple. First, we have to protect all people who worked with and for him/her from any authorities who may wish to do them harm. Second, it wouldn't do to fully investigate an affair that might affect the future release of information regarding our existence. These are the rules I am establishing before I inform you of these historic facts about the Republican Party nomination. Now let's get on with this nomination report.

When Bari finally registered to run as a candidate for the Republican Party, we noticed that the 2012 presidential season had a total of 390 candidates, and most of these people were unknown to the vast majority of Americans. How could we ensure that we were included in the debates with the top candidates?

Even though Bari had been in the Republican Party for a while, he wasn't known at all at the higher levels, so we made him out to be a successful person. This appeared to be quite feasible since it was nothing unusual for successful people to run for office.

As I mentioned before, I am not going to identify the human name that was used for Bari Tone . . . yet! We will do this a little later when our relationship with humans gets rolling so to speak. In the meantime, our worst fears were realized when our candidate was not included in the televised debates, and we couldn't figure out why.

We asked him for a complete analysis of what he thought was happening. Bari thought there was a conspiracy among the upper members of the party to keep the lower ones out. We listened to all the recordings he secretly made of sessions among party members at their meetings. When Bari asked them why the vast majority of candidates were not on television, he didn't get much in convincing answers. They told him there were too many candidates and only the most well known ones would be acceptable.

Nevertheless, we were determined not to repeat the same mistakes as in our last experience in the 1970s. The big difference this time was that we were opting for a U.S. presidential candidate and forgetting about other countries for now.

Our campaign created a website discussing the main issues of the day (again the website name will not be disclosed; it has since been withdrawn). Since we were running as 'right-wing' Republicans, right wing issues like the following were purposely promoted:

208

- we must get our people to be better Christians.
- we've got to lower taxes to get America back on a roll.
- liberals are destroying our country.
- unions are destroying our country.
- we are being infiltrated by Muslims.
- God bless Ronald Reagan.

We didn't necessarily believe in all of the above but did consider changing and improving them to give us an edge. So here is what we came up with.

- only Christians and maybe only ministers to rule America.
- no taxes and possibly even give money away.
- outlaw liberalism.
- outlaw unions.
- outlaw Muslims.
- God bless only Republicans.

Next thing to do was set up a campaign office headquarter and hire staff. We appointed Regintians in cloned bodies for the top echelon of the staff except for the campaign manager -- as usual, he won't be named. I had made the decision to be one of those staff people along with one more person from the local Explorer Station, named Turner. Some advantages we had were Bari's superb memory compared with humans. If he needed to remember any debate points, he had no trouble there.

Finally, the big moment came; Bari had to give his first major speech announcing his candidacy. We rented an auditorium in an old theater scheduled for demolition. The purpose was to demonstrate that our candidate could spend money wisely, since this rental didn't cost us very much. We thought Republicans would be impressed with that.

On the day Bari and his entourage showed up to give the speech in that auditorium, it had exactly three people. One was the janitor/guard (on his last day there since the building was scheduled to be demolished the very next day), the other one has a person who was related to one of the people on our staff, and the third one was a reporter for a local newspaper. I must admit Bari was upset and confused. He had an argument with his campaign manager. The problem was a result of Bari's insistence of spending as little money as possible, so he could brag to the press and fellow Republicans on how well he could manage it.

This confused the hell out of the staff, as they thought Bari was going to spend his own money on promoting the speech that evening, and he thought his own people, with whatever funds they had, would do it. The result was that word never got out to the press other than that lone reporter who was actually a summer student working as a junior reporter for that newspaper.

Well another argument ensued as to whether the speech should even be given considering the lack of people in there. The campaign manager said, "Just go ahead and I'll record the speech on my cell camcorder and make sure not to aim it at the audience" (or lack of it), "then I'll doctor it enough so that it looks like nothing untoward has happened. Then we'll release it on YouTube and our campaign website."

So here is the speech written and spoken by Bari Tone.

"My fellow Americans and Republicans: God bless me and of course, you people in the audience and all around our country. I am a true Christian, a believer in capitalism, a fighter against socialism like those Democrats, a believer in our God given constitution, a deficit fighter, a believer in the right to bear arms of any type, a believer that global warming is a conspiracy by communists to eventually prevent the worship of our Christian God. I am pledging to you that not only will I prevent taxes from going up; I will ensure that they'll go down. I will keep a very close eye on all liberals and Democrats to make sure they don't allow Muslims to infiltrate us, unions to destroy us, and Ivy League professors to destroy our economy. God bless Ronald Regan."

It was a very brief speech and there was total silence at the end of it . . .

Well, not exactly total silence; you could hear a dog barking down the street, and farther away a truck picking up garbage.

Later that evening, we had a meeting about our total mismanagement of the situation. After all the analysis and study of politics that have been done since our democratic run, we felt confident about doing the right things this time, but when we went ahead and did it, it was a usually a major screw up.

Something had to be done. The obvious thing would be to get rid of Bari, but he was my son, and I promised I'd stick with him till the end.

Then someone had a fantastic idea; I have to admit that at first I thought it was crazy. This might sound unbelievable, but here it is: 'Abduct one of the major candidates', and I mean major -- one of the top seven. Replace him/her with a cloned copy. In other words, use the same body, but remove his/her brain and replace it with Bari's. Copy all of his/her brain data containing his/her memories, and place it in Bari's brain (since Regintians have a lot of room). He/she would then take orders from us because it would be Bari controlling that human body.

Now I would like to urge you humans who are reading this section, to calm down, especially if you're a Republican. I promise you that we did not mean any harm to any of these candidates, and I will explain why. Once we got our man/woman into the White House, we would remove our person's brain and replace him/her with the original person's brain and place a few thoughts into his/her mind that will welcome our announcements.

See, that's all we would do, no reason to be frightened or get upset.

After discussing this for a few minutes, we all agreed it was a brilliant plan. From another point of view, why wouldn't we just replace everyone in government with our clones and then control everything?

The problem is risk management. A replacement clone has a failure probability of about 1%. This means that the more people are abducted and replace with clones, the greater the chance of being discovered. It's better to place one clone into a high value position then having many all over the place without the assurance that they can be controlled 100% of the time. We have done abducting, clone replacing, and re-substituting in the past, but only in emergencies. We are here to study you after all, not control you.

So that's what we ended up doing. Obviously, I won't tell you who it is because I don't want to make the life of that person miserable. I want him/her to continue with his/her normal life. It wasn't easy abducting this person without anyone knowing. Staff, family, and security people constantly surrounded that person, so he/she was very difficult to approach.

Several methods considered for abducting the candidate were:

If the person is catholic, wait until he/she goes to confession and then have the confessor (one of our clones again) take over the confessee's body, so when the candidate leaves he/she will have the implanted brain in his/her head.

What if the person is not catholic and even if he/she was, might not have sins on their soul (or don't believe they have) and won't need to go?

Since most of these candidates are wealthy, they might take the odd holiday in the Caribbean (not necessarily the Cayman Islands) which would reduce the number of people surrounding the person and thus increase our chance of abduction.

Most candidates have a Super PAC supporting them. We thought of creating our own Super PAC, loading it with millions of dollars, demanding a meeting with the candidate (after all Super PAC personnel do have secret meetings from time to time), then an abduction opportunity might present itself.

The last and most plausible idea is to have one of those TV evangelists lure the candidate into their church headquarters, publicly endorse him/her, take him/her out to a backroom where prayers are said and ideas are exchanged and when the person walks out of there, it will be with their new brain -- smiling and waving of course.

Once again, I can't reveal which of the above techniques were used; we wish to keep everything as secret as possible.

As time went on, this project became one of the most nerve-wracking experiences we've ever had. The pressure not to screw up was enormous. When our clone finally took over the body of our designated candidate, we constantly reviewed everything our clone did and said, and analyzed it for anything that might hinder our goals. Mistakes were made, dumb things said, blunders done, but the only reason no one suspected anything went wrong with our candidate was that the other 'non-abducted' candidates behavior were as erratic as our own with a total lack of distinguishment (not sure if that's a real word).

Another consideration was deciding how religious our candidate should be. The initial rounds of debate in the Iowa caucuses forced us to appear religious, to the point where we might be turning off mainstream Americans.

Then suddenly, the regular primaries appear, and one has to de-religify (is that the correct word?), and then other primaries in the south happen and one has to re-religify. It was bonkers.

Oh yes, and then there are the slogans. You might already be familiar with most of them. Let's check some of the most standard conservative ones out there.

- A pregnancy resulting from rape is actually a 'gift from God'.
- It's Not Really Fascism When Christians do it.
- Submission & Obedience to husbands.
- All of America's Problems are due to Godlessness and Godless liberals.
- Criticism of Religions is not free speech.
- Thank God for George W. Bush: Christian Nationalists Believe Bush Was Chosen by God, not the People.

NOTE: Our expedition's leader attempted to contact God to find out if this was true, and the Spirit Congregation told us that God refused to answer.

Whenever Bari stated any of the above slogans, he was surprisingly complimented. At this point, it was obvious that aligning ourselves with this conservative philosophy could create an excellent shot at winning the election. Our association with the radical left years ago taught us a lesson: do not go to extremes; American society never goes that far. Who was joining this conservative movement?

Our observations indicated a lot of the mainstream public were becoming part of it. It was obvious this conservative approach would never go away. Since most of these slogans were being produced by conservatives, we got together with our 'cloned candidate' (with Bari's brain in it of course) and produced what we thought would be our own special slogans that would get us attention and votes. In addition, Bari went over every one of Sarah Palin's speeches and quotes to get ideas.

Here are five of her quotes along with the inspiration we received from them:

"The America I know and love is not one in which my parents or my baby with Down Syndrome will have to stand in front of Obama's 'death panel' so his bureaucrats can decide, based on a subjective judgment of their 'level of productivity in society,' whether they are worthy of health care. Such a system is downright evil."

Our own inspired quote -- All Obama death panels will be replaced by free-enterprise death panels.

" 'Refudiate,' 'misunderestimate,' 'wee-wee'd up.' English is a living language. Shakespeare liked to coin new words too. Got to celebrate it! "

Our own inspired quote -- *'geekation', 'de-religify', 're-religify', 'distinguishment'* are now OK to use.

"But obviously, we've got to stand with our North Korean allies."

Our own inspired quote -- *Damn those liberals, we've got to stand with our North Korean allies.*

"We used to hustle over the border for health care we received in Canada."

Our candidate's position is to treat Canada both as if it were a supplier of medical health care and a private business. Then we'd get the best of both worlds: Sarah Palin's approval on obtaining medical health care in Canada, and then getting our own insurance companies to pay Canadian health care fees as if it were a free-enterprise company.

"Polls are for strippers and cross-country skiers"

It took us a while to understand this and when we did, we came up with, "Polls are for strippers when they submit to their husbands."

The above Palin quotes were a true inspiration. The next thing to do was produce our own quotes based on these commonly used conservative slogans. We would now call:

'a pregnancy resulting from rape is a gift from God' replaced with:

> 'A pregnancy resulting from rape an *Award from God.*''

'It's not really fascism when Christians do it' replaced with:

> 'If Christian's don't do it, it could be communism.'

'Submission & Obedience to husbands' is now:

> 'Submission & Obedience to Husbands AND BOYFRIENDS.'

'All of America's Problems are Due to Godlessness and Godless Liberals' replaced by:

> 'All of America's Problems are Due to Godlessness and Godless Liberals and their ability to brainwash college graduates.'

'Criticism of Religion is Not Free Speech' is to be replaced by:

> 'Criticism of Christians is Not Free Speech'

And finally:

> 'Thank God for George W. Bush, after all he was chosen by God.'

God still wouldn't co-operate with us to confirm this, so we're replacing it with:

> 'Thank God for Vice President Cheney, God endowed him to be a steady rifle-republican.

We thought the above points were brilliant until Turner (the other Regintian on the campaign staff), who had actually (and very wisely) studied all the history of the human race, told us otherwise in a meeting.

When he saw our list of quotes for the first time . . . let's just say he had a certain type of body language that is difficult to describe in human terms since our bodies are so different than yours. As we squatted in the meeting room (as a reminder, we don't sit, we squat), he glared at us as if we were inexperienced little children.

Since Bari Tone was the one to 'finalize' the list, he spoke to him first, "Bari, do you know what a death panel is?"

Bari, being a bit of a buffoon, was just about to answer in a sarcastic way, but I interrupted him wanting to avoid a heated discussion.

So I said, "What difference does it make since Sarah Palin said it. We are following her inspiration because of her popularity right now."

"Right . . . Ooook . . . ah . . . how do I explain this? I don't believe that quote should be used in the context that you put it in. The bad part in the phrase 'Obama death panel' were the words 'death panel', not 'Obama'. The North Koreans are not American allies, it's the South Koreans."

Even I knew that. OK I could see his point; maybe we assumed that because Sarah said all these things, there was nothing to worry about. I began wondering whether we might be screwing up interpretations just as we did in the 70s, and miscalculating everything.

Bari was adamant that we should leave everything in the list as it was, but eventually relented on the two points Turner had made on the death panels and Korean allies. All the other buffoonery on the list was left alone. No one wanted to argue with Bari.

The next step was to get together with the original Earth campaign staff (the human part of it) to see what they thought about the list. It took place on a Friday night the day before a major debate.

During the meeting, our candidate -- now with Bari's brain -- addressed the campaign manager with the presence of the staff, "Bill, I've just put together some carefully worded comments and slogans that I feel can really propel and inspire our existing supporters and add a lot of new ones. Maybe you and the staff can fine tune them and determine what the best way is of getting them out there."

Bill took the copies from the candidate (Bari) and handed them out to the rest of the staff. There was complete silence as everyone read his own copy.

Someone spoke up, "Boy this is real funny, but you know with that debate tomorrow night we don't have enough time for this right now, so we should get on with a debate strategy."

The manager knew our candidate well enough to know he/she was serious. Uncertainties between the manager and the candidate were growing as if the manager was noticing a change in the candidate's personality. We were hoping our clone was adopting the original personality well enough so that no one would notice, but we were never too sure.

"Are you serious about this or is this just a joke."

Bari was just about to mention that he embraced these slogans wholeheartedly but at the last second had second thoughts. Why were the staff people staring at our candidate so strangely; did they like the slogans or not -- or maybe just a few? I could feel Bari churning things over in his mind.

He compromised and said, "I thought I'd throw in a few funny ones just to lighten things up since this has been a stressful week."

The manager was the first to speak out and asked very slowly, "So which ones are the humorous ones?"

Bari was now feeling the pressure and thought he had better be careful, or he might lose a bit of support here. I later found out that it wasn't just the manager who was noticing something unusual in our candidate, there was gossip among the rest of the staff as to whether the candidate was losing his sanity.

"Ha, ha, ha, you guys are paranoid. Come on, it's obvious which ones are jokes. You guys gotta be kidding, ha ha ha." Bari by this time wasn't sure which to admit were jokes or not.

Even though Regintians don't have a sense of humor, after studying human's humor for centuries, we thought we could understand most of it. The problem of course was our inability to come up with our own jokes. So here is our candidate believing these slogans would get everyone's approval but now had to decide how to interpret 'some' as jokes to placate doubts among his staff as to whether he was bonkers.

"Let's just forget about these things for now. I know we're pretty busy, so let's get down to tomorrow's debate."

There was a bit of silence as people started shuffling paper around.

Someone said, "OK let's come up with a prayer that will assure victory. Get one of those pocket bibles and make sure it's next to your heart."

They were obviously making fun of the candidate. Bari realized their respect was gradually wearing away. In the debate the following evening, he/she was either going to lose or gain more respect, but there was a general feeling that this might be the end of it.

I watched the debate from the audience, and overall I was pleased that our candidate didn't behave foolishly. But he/she didn't exactly stand out either. Even though our cloning technology was advanced, there comes a point in time where we realize that the tiny nuances of personality 'distinguishment' are almost impossible to reproduce: another note to enter into our storehouse of knowledge of humans.

After a while, we decided to pull Bari's brain out and return the original abducted human's brain back to his/her normal body. We collected all the main memories of the campaign, injected them back into the original candidate's memory cells, and then release him/her. We kept an eye on him/her for a while to confirm that he/she was fully recovered and none too wise about what really happened to him/her.

Overall, our plan was a complete failure. Then Obama won the election, which made our attempt to invest our time in a right wing ideology appear inept. I don't think that we'll ever attempt it again; politics is just too confusing . . . for Regintians.

FINAL DECISION ON WHAT TO DO

It's Appleton again. We are not going to participate in any more political campaigns, abductions or insertions, and the continuing discussion of how and when to reveal ourselves has resulted in three possible methods:

1. Descend in our spaceships, land in specific areas, then take over the airways and introduce ourselves. This methodology was used in bad sci-fi movies over the years and not only did it scare the hell out of humans in those movies, it would also scare us if anything went wrong.

2. Introduce ourselves behind the scenes to the major powers like the United States of America or Russia and/or the European Union and China. This is tricky. Although we have studied human culture for thousands of years, we thought we had a handle on human understanding. But along comes the 20th century with the widespread use of democracy and the global village concept of spreading information. So how do we approach these governments: one at a time, all at once? Would they feel threatened by us or be awestruck? These are things we have to consider or maybe neither of us has that maturity.

3. The third way is writing this book.

When the idea first surfaced, it was considered wacky. Sort of thing you would find in an American sitcom. The more we thought about it, the more we realized its potential as a reasonable proposition. I have to admit it *was* my idea, and I put a lot of pressure on our management people until they began to see its potential.

As you stand here in our museum in an avatar, along with holding in your hand the results of this effort, we hope you are able to appreciate the honesty and sincerity of what is happening. After millions of people have read it, we will announce a time and place where we will officially descend and invite qualified leaders into our vessels.

In the meantime, this idea produced a couple of other problems: how to write it and how to publish it. It is something that no one has had any experience with whatsoever. When one approaches a publisher with the things we desire to publish, how would they react to the fact that we are aliens from a far distant star system? Would they believe it? Would we have to take them into outer space and demonstrate our technology?

Yes, these visits have been real, and there has been an attempted cover up. The real surprise though, is that the cover-up hasn't been as a result of deviousness by the U.S. and other governments, but by us -- the UFO aliens. I know. I was one of the people who infiltrated the U.S. government to ensure they weren't aware of what was really going on.

Before I began writing this book, I was always the Regintian who casually worked as a simple government worker in a variety of U.S. government departments. I did not interfere in anything or recorded things audibly or visually. I spent one year each, in eight departments starting in 2003.

The job I remembered the most was working in the White House. Now I know what you're thinking. If I'm working in the White House, I must have had access to all kinds of secret documents and things similar to that. No, I was merely a clerk in an area that wasn't even in the main building. But the important thing was what I learned, not only about human nature, but also human political nature in the United States.

I did manage on one occasion to be near President Obama, Hillary Clinton and Joe Biden. It was in August 2012 and was one of the few times that I happened to be over in the main White House building. The rumors around the political universe at the time was that Obama was contemplating getting rid of Biden and replacing him with Clinton. I could observe from their interactions that it was not likely to happen.

That evening, when I went back to my apartment, I got a call from Bari and he asks me, "I noticed you were physically close to Obama and his vice-president. What do you think of replacing Biden with a cloned version of either me or you?"

I wasn't exactly expecting a question like this, considering we had finally dropped the whole issue of abducting and cloning. I hesitated a bit when I answered him. I have to admit that being close to important people presents us with insertion opportunities and quite frankly, Vice-President Biden might have been the best candidate for us to clone. I mean if a cloned version of Biden were to say something ignorant, dim-witted or flaky, the press would report it as another standard Biden gaffe and not compromise our secret in any way.

"I'll have to think about it. Let's discuss this idea in our next meeting this weekend."

We both hung up, and later had our meeting in a secret location in Washington D.C. Bari and I were present, along with Turner, and the Earth expedition leader.

Bari started off, "Well don't you think this is a great idea. I mean the biggest problem we've had has been our naïve views not only on humor, but we can never figure out the limits of how radical we should be on religion because we don't adapt to human subtleties very well. With us in there as Biden, no one would notice the difference if our clone would say or do something really dumb. It's the perfect position."

I said, "Bari, I have to admit, since you brought this idea up I have given it some thought. The problem is that we've lost our momentum to abduct and clone people. Every plan we've devised always began with high hopes, but we were eventually disappointed. Is this going to be another one of these situations?"

We all stared at Turner waiting for his opinion. He sat there stone faced. He'd been through this before, and it didn't appear that he approved this suggestion.

"The problem is not with the idea. The problem is the people you're sending down there to do the work. I wish we had a real intelligent 'Regintian' human for an agent that has grown up in the U.S. That would be the perfect candidate."

This time our Earth expedition leader spoke up. "Turner, what about you? You have such an incredible knowledge of all things human including their sense of humor, purpose, destiny, and many other characteristics, that I think you are not likely to bumble anything if you were to become the clone for Biden."

He definitely had a point there. Turner was smart, didn't have a massive ego (ala Bari), and knew minute human detail not only in history but in cultural matters as well.

His answer, "Ahhhh . . . welllll . . . errrrr."

The above is a translation of course. It's impossible to directly translate these types of responses from the Regintian language, which is based on the electromagnetic spectrum, to audible words from a human's mouth, but that's the best I could do.

Turner continued, "What's wrong with my initial suggestion. What we could do is send a cloned couple with cloned children to live in Washington D.C. Send them to school from elementary to college so that they would be completely adapted into Earth culture, and then you might have the right kind of people to do these things."

It was too late of course. We didn't fancy to waiting for these clones to be integrated into human society. It was obvious that Turner didn't want anything to do with this proposal. Bari yearned to do it, but our experience with him hadn't been very rewarding these past few years. And personally, I had no time to do this since I was writing this book.

So there you have it, as of November 2012, a completely Regintian free political structure in the United States of America.

But let's get on with ending this museum tour. You might have noticed other avatars from Earth as you've been wandering around. Unfortunately, you will not be able to communicate with them for the time being. There are still problems with verbalizing communications among these present models. I will now direct you out of the museum and give you instructions on what to do next.

Please, this way out the back door. Now that we're outside, have a seat here in the garden and remove your fingers from the book. After you've done that, you will regain consciousness back on Earth in the exact place you were when you started reading this book. It has been a pleasure meeting you and introducing you to this incredible situation, and I am sure we shall meet again in the future.

So long and thanks for all the patience.

ADDENDUM-DON'T FORGET TO READ THIS

I would like to apologize for the following. I have already published this book, and I had to add this addendum. For those of you who bought the first edition of this book that doesn't contain this addendum, I am reprogramming the nanobots inside those books so that when they are read, a warning message will be sent into the minds of those people. The message will urge them to go back into the museum with their avatars to catch up on this addendum.

Here is the problem. The Reginta Brotherhood has released me of my membership. This is the central authority of Reginta. The reason is simple; they are claiming that I have been so indoctrinated into Earth culture that I am more or less a de-facto member of your planet. They have told me to leave your planet and have forbidden me from ever going back to it. At this point in time, I am currently residing on Earth and have no intention of ever leaving. Because of this situation, I am seeking refuge on this world and plan to seek the most influential people on the planet to offer me refuge. The first person I thought of was the president of the United States, but he is so surrounded by secret service people it might be difficult to penetrate. The Reginta authorities have remotely disabled all the advanced technology afforded me in communicating with practically anybody I wish for.

I was also going to contact Vladimir Putin and/or the Russian authorities but came across the same problem. I also thought of other important leaders throughout the world, but am also considering either Steven Spielberg or George Lucas or maybe even Bill Gates.

On the odd occasion when I went back to Reginta, I brought some habits along that I had become used to while living on Earth. I always wanted to play music (something which doesn't exist in Reginta and is considered extremely annoying), tried to maintain my human cloned body (they find humans extremely ugly), and inadvertently used audible communications by mistake (which made me appear somewhat eccentric).

In the meantime, I am searching for a place to live that will hide me from the Brotherhood. Sorry for having to end this book so abruptly, I don't know what is going to happen to it since its publication will be removed from my hands sometime in the near future.

NOTICE: 2nd ADDENDUM - PLEASE READ THIS AS WELL

I have decided to add yet another addendum. The same conditions still apply as the first one. There has definitely been a 'Command to seize' issued by the Reginta Brotherhood to prevent me from exposing our visits to Earth prematurely, that is to say before they give full approval. I realize that I have not been telling you the complete truth. I was so eager to publish this book, I implied the Reginta authorities were approving its release.

There is a debate going on as to whether releasing it was a good idea. Many people in the Brotherhood are against it. They claim that humans are still not ready for this. I disagree. You people are definitely ready, and I believe this dispute is something to do with Reginta politics or a struggle for power going on behind the scenes or something similar.

I am officially in hiding. While I don't believe they will kill me, they will certainly take over my mind and reprogram it. It is very difficult to hide from them since they can detect me with flying nanobots even though I resemble a regular human. I am now residing in a major city in the United States in a lovely apartment and have taken means to prevent those nanobots from detecting me.

NOTICE: 3rd ADDENDUM

Earthling, they are now searching for me, and I cannot continue to be your host. I thought I could evade their nanobots, but I believe they have found me. That means that you and I have to cease communications. I am going to issue you a new avatar so that you can visit our heaven. Don't worry, the communications will be instantaneous, this is the spirit world after all. Just hang on for now and do not remove your fingers from the book or you might miss the link.

. . . .

.

.

Ugh

.

.

.

NOTICE: 4th ADDENDUM

Brrrrrrrr.........................

Ting.....................................
sptow..sptow..sptow..sptow..

..

Blub ..de..blub..de..blub..de..blub..de..blub....... ?[1]

Ah...
hello?

Oh! . . . . . .
Er . . .

Greetings Earthling.

You must be another one of those Earthlings that was sent here by Appleton. I hope you can communicate with me. So far, no one has said a word.

OK go ahead and say something.

. . .
Well I'm waiting . . .

OK do this. Instead of sitting down in a chair or lying on a sofa, please stand up. Yes, you heard me; stand up. It will clear your mind and allow you to communicate. OK? Now assuming you are standing up, I want you to do this. Configure your right hand so that the two middle fingers are curled up, your index finger and little finger are

---

[1] - spirit noise and static. Unfortunately, we were not able to filter this out with either passive or active filters but will include an existential filter in future editions.

extended, and your thumb is at right angles. If you have the paperback version of this book, you will now point the index and little finger in towards the edges of the pages with your thumb pointing down.

If you have an electronic book, then curl your fingers up in a fist except for your index finger and its neighbor. Now place the back of your hand to the back of the electronic book and allow the two extended fingers to be pointing upwards.

OK, just wait for about five seconds, and we should be able to communicate. . .

. . .

Still haven't heard anything from you.

. . .

Try speaking out loud instead of thinking.

. . .

If you happen to be standing in the middle of a floor in a café like Starbucks, I understand your dilemma. It would be a bit embarrassing to be talking in the middle of this place with your hand connected to this book in the manner that I have suggested.

Try this, get in line to buy something and when the clerk asks for your order, then start talking to me. The only person who might think you're crazy would be the clerk: hey but at least it's only one person and not the rest of the people around you.

There might be another reason for your inability to communicate and that is you think my request is a big joke or is really dumb. I can assure you I am being very serious. If you don't want to be embarrassed because you happened to be in a café or on a bus, then just wait until you get home and try it again.

Assuming you are in a comfortable place, let's try it now . . .

OK one more time . . .

Still nothing. I still can't hear you. Oh well, you're not the first Earthling that I couldn't communicate with and probably won't be the last. Let's get on with this effort.

Assuming that you can understand me without any problems, I will continue with my little schpeal. Let's discuss religion. This particular religion of ours encompasses all the present and pass religions of Earth as well as those on Reginta.

First of all, as you already know, Regintians are not required to worship anyone in the spirit world. Second, unlike your religions, which allow you to visit your spiritual world only after you die, Regintians are physically allowed to visit us if they don't mind the ~250 year travel time to and back. The other way of getting here is either by dying, assuming you have no mortal sins on your soul spreadsheet, or by visiting with an avatar.

However, we are giving every human who buys this book a special privilege (think of it as a heavenly discount). Appleton has told you in that last addendum that you are currently visiting heaven right now.

This is not quite accurate. You happen to be standing in the foyer to heaven. It use to be called the 'Pearly Gates', but since we underwent renovations about ten years ago, we changed the name to 'iCloud' (our legal department has already contacted Apple Inc.).

You're currently allowed one visit to heaven with the avatar you're presently using. At this very moment, the waiting period is anywhere from 2 weeks to 200 years and if you put this book down, it effectively puts you at the back of the line. We happen to be behind in our production of avatars due to the incredible sales of this book. It has caused a huge demand for avatars to visit our museum and has extended the waiting period for visitors to heaven. So just think of this line-up as our form of purgatory. We will keep track of the time you spend in this waiting line and subtract it in the form of venial sin accumulation from your soul spreadsheet. A long waiting period is a form of suffering is it not. This of course makes our purgatory unique. Its occupation is not based on the amount of sins on your soul but on the efficiency of our avatar production line.

Once again, you have to hold your book in the manner I described anywhere from 2 weeks to 200 years or wait longer if you put it down.

Good-Luck!

NOTICE: 5th ADDENDUM
(hopefully the last one)

Dear Earthling,

This is Massage DeMessuer, head of the Brotherhood organization on the planet Reginta. I have some bad news for you but some good news for us: Appleton has finally been apprehended. We will not be making any formal announcements regarding our visits to Earth. Just continue to believe it is nothing more than a pseudoscience (like palm reading or astrology).

If you have already told people about Appleton's book and that it is a way of announcing our relationship to Earthlings over many years, just tell them you were joking. It is the only choice you have. We will not be sending our spaceships to orbit your planet or using messages to take over your airways and because of that, people might think you are crazy when you mention you have been communicating with aliens.

Yes, there might be a time in the future when we will make definite contact with your entire planet. But not on this day or this time.

You may now remove your fingers from the book and the nanobots will automatically retire.

Oh, one more thing, we cannot offer any refunds for this book even though it did not achieve the intention of its author, Appleton. The cost of supplying the nanobots and avatars far exceeds the revenues of this book, so you should understand our position and realize that we are being very sensible.

Thank you Earthling and best wishes.

Massage DeMessuer.

PS: In case you have an inquiry about joining our religion, I am afraid that Earthlings are not permitted. The

God person in that religion (which was actually the greeter you were talking to in the previous addendum), was not impressed.

50,000 A.D. The Awakening

What happens when a person from the 21st century wakes up 50,000 years in the future?

You might say that Henry Matthews is the luckiest man in the universe. By pure chance, in 2012, his head along with all his thoughts and memories were protected and preserved, allowing him to stay alive for 50,000 years.

- What does this future hold?
- Total peace?
- Long life?
- Enlightened Democracy?

. . . or something else.

50,000 years in the future,

Henry Matthews is ready to begin an adventure of great discovery.

What does this future think of him?

Since their own ancient record of human existence only goes back 35,000 years, trillions of people are now waiting to discover this lost history when Henry awakens. However, some refuse to believe human history is older than 35,000 years, so that could only mean one thing. Henry Matthews must be something other than a human being.

. . . but what?

This novel also tries to establish some relationships between 'ancient' and 'new' by comparing a few aspects of the different cultures and languages that you would expect to change over these vast periods of time: does the hero of the story manage to figure out what the new languages he encounters evolved from?

PART 1 - How Henry Matthews finds his way to 50,000 A.D.

PART 2 - How he is discovered and what anxiety and/or thrills it causes in these future societies in both a political and spiritual way.

PART 3 - Henry is revived and his relationship to this new era is exposed.

PART 4 - Opps! sorry no spoilers (but you will be intrigued by what happens).

youtube promo video: youtu.be/hALUeaaRsgQ

(j-jack-bergeron.com)

Printed in Poland
by Amazon Fulfillment
Poland Sp. z o.o., Wrocław